THE UNLISTED

BOOK THREE – SABOTAGE

THE *UNLISTED*

BOOK THREE – SABOTAGE

JUSTINE FLYNN   CHRIS KUNZ

LOTHIAN
Children's Books

A Lothian Children's Book

Published in Australia and New Zealand in 2019
by Hachette Australia
Level 17, 207 Kent Street, Sydney NSW 2000
www.hachettechildrens.com.au

10 9 8 7 6 5 4 3 2 1

 A catalogue record for this
book is available from the
NATIONAL National Library of Australia
LIBRARY
OF AUSTRALIA

ISBN: 978 0 7344 1959 0 (paperback)

Cover design by Kinart
Cover photographs courtesy of Aquarius Films
Text design by Bookhouse, Sydney
Typeset in 12.5/19.4 pt Garamond MT Pro by Bookhouse, Sydney
Printed and bound in Australia by McPherson's Printing Group

Dedicated to the young people who are brave enough to question the status quo – the future belongs to you

It was mid-morning in the Sharma house. Identical Indian–Australian twins Kal and Dru entered the kitchen, coming face to face with an old man, who looked a bit like their father. He was seated at the kitchen table, which was covered with brushes, powders and other make-up. Their older sister, Vidya, was picking up a make-up brush from a pouch when she turned and saw her brothers' faces.

Using his best grandpa voice, Rahul asked, 'How do you like your old man?'

Their confused expressions made their sister and father laugh.

Dru looked to Vidya. 'You did this?'

'Why are you so surprised?' asked Vidya. 'I've been studying stage make-up all year. And Dad's being my model for my character assignment which is due tomorrow.'

Kal peered up close at Rahul. 'It's good how you've managed to make Dad look really ancient,' he said, impressed.

'Really ancient but also really handsome, no?' said Rahul with a gleam in his eye.

Dadi bustled around the kitchen, filling a tiffin with prepared food. 'Why waste your talent making my son look so old? Why not make your dadi look young?'

Vidya knew exactly what to say in a situation like this. 'But Dadi – people already think you're my sister!'

Dadi smiled at her granddaughter but then, just as quickly, frowned. 'Can you believe they're making my poor daughter work all weekend? Dru, I'll need your help to take your bua's lunch to her.'

The twins' aunt, a doctor, had recently started working for the Global Child Initiative (GCI), which she had thought was a wonderful organisation created to help children receive the best health care available, all around the world. But the shady parent company Infinity Group was behind the Initiative, and rather than altruistic aims, something much more sinister had come into play. The GCI rolled out 'dental checks' to schools all over Australia – it wasn't a normal dental check though. Infinity Group had used the appointments to implant every child with a device that could be tracked, giving the company the ability to know where every implanted child was at any given time, and – even more frighteningly – to influence their thoughts and actions.

Dru and Kal were some of the only people aware of what was really going on, all because of Dru's terror of the dentist. He had convinced his brother to pretend to be him for the check-up, not realising that this meant Kal had been implanted twice.

When the students at Westbrook High started to behave strangely – group loss of consciousness, increased strength and enhanced language skills – Dru and Kal had started to investigate what was really going on.

Because Dru hadn't been implanted, he was not being brainwashed like his brother and all the other kids in their class. Through their investigative work the twins had discovered other 'Unlisted' kids who had not gone to the dental check-up or received the implant. The twins had befriended four runaways – Kymara, Rose, Jacob and Gemma – who had been hiding out in the tunnels of St James train station, and had helped them as much as they could. But Rose had been captured and was now imprisoned at GCI headquarters, which was where the twins' dadi was suggesting they go for a nice Sunday outing to see their aunt.

'Oh, you hear that, Kal?' Dru said. 'A trip to Global Child Initiative headquarters.'

Kal shrugged, non-committal.

'Maybe we should both go,' suggested Dru with a meaningful look at his twin. Dru needed Kal near him at headquarters because otherwise they might find out he wasn't being tracked.

'Sure,' said Kal, unenthused.

'Both my wombats! What a treat,' said Dadi. 'Kal, please fetch the umbrellas.'

Kal looked out the window. The sun was shining. 'But there's not a cloud in the sky.'

'Believe your dadi,' she said in her wise-woman voice. 'A storm is coming.'

Dru swallowed hard at his grandmother's ominous words.

•

Dadi drove the two boys into the city, and they were soon at the front entrance of GCI headquarters. The twins had been there a few days earlier with their school group, taking part in an organised scavenger hunt – but the results weren't exactly what the GCI official had planned, with another Unlisted boy, a Chinese exchange student named Jiao, being captured and taken away. These were not good memories, and the boys weren't happy to be back again so soon.

Dadi looked up, oblivious to the boys' discomfort. 'My, my, look at this impressive building, boys,' she said. 'If you work hard at school, you might be able to get a job in a place like this too.'

The boys shared a horrified look. This was literally the last place they would want to work. Ever.

Dadi, wearing a bright sari, bustled through the entrance towards the metal detector until she was stopped by a security guard. The tiffins were metal and had to be checked separately.

'What's this?' asked the security guard suspiciously.

Dadi pulled out the tiffin. 'Lunch for my daughter, of course,' she said indignantly. 'She's working. On a Sunday.'

'She's not the only one,' said the guard unsympathetically.

Kal and Dru passed through the metal detector together.

'Open the lunch, please,' instructed the guard.

The boys noticed a second security guard holding a handheld implant scanner, stationed near the stairs.

Dadi opened the first compartment of the tiffin. A delicious aroma rose from the still-warm samosas.

The security guard sighed. 'That smells sensational. I'm supposed to be on a diet, but –'

'Take one,' Dadi said graciously. 'I have plenty.'

The guard did not need to be asked twice. He grabbed a samosa and bit into it, moaning in appreciation as Dadi opened a small container of raita. 'And this is my special mint chutney.'

The guard dipped his samosa in the chutney before popping it in his mouth. 'Oh, even better.'

He waved Dadi through the scanner, and she and the twins approached the reception desk, passing a small group of adults seated in the foyer.

Dadi said to the receptionist, 'Could you please tell Dr Sharma her mother and nephews are here with her lunch?'

The receptionist nodded and called Maya Sharma's extension. While they were waiting, a middle-aged woman with a blonde bob, wearing a white shirt and black trousers approached the reception desk. 'Hello. I'm here for the Super Recogniser training day.'

The receptionist gestured to the other seated adults. 'Wait over there with the others,' she instructed.

Dru's attention was caught by a screen that displayed images of missing children along with the text: *Have you seen these children? Every child deserves a better future.*

Dru looked at Kal and nodded to the screen. Kal shrugged. 'We're here to find out about Rose. Don't lose focus.'

Maya appeared in the foyer, looking weary and drawn.

'Oh my girl,' said Dadi sympathetically. 'You look so tired. Luckily, I've brought you a nutritious lunch.'

'Thank you, Mum,' said Maya, giving her a hug. 'Hello boys.' She gave them a lingering, pointed look, and Kal immediately took the hint.

'Dadi,' he said, 'I think that guard looks like he'd really like another samosa. You should give him one.'

'Good idea, my wombat,' said Dadi with a grin. She picked up one with a serviette and walked with Kal over to the guard, who greeted Dadi like a long-lost relative when he saw what she was bringing him.

Maya quietly relayed the information she knew Dru would be desperate to hear. 'Your friends tried to escape last night. But Emma Ainsworth brought them back in.'

'What? Where are they keeping them?' asked Dru.

'Level one,' answered Maya before frowning. 'Don't even think about it, Dru. I'll figure something out. But there's something else I need to . . .' She lost her train of thought as she noticed the Super Recognisers. Concern flashed across her face.

Dru followed her gaze. 'What's the matter, Bua? Who are they?'

'They're called Super Recognisers. They're people who've been tested and found to have a natural ability to recall any face in an instant. The Initiative plans to hire hundreds of them.'

'Why?' asked Dru.

'They're determined to find every child who missed the dental check – these Super Recognisers will help track them down.'

Dru was horrified, but there was no time to say anything else as Dadi returned with Kal. 'Let's go, boys. I can feel that storm getting closer.'

After saying goodbye to Maya, Dru, Kal and Dadi headed back outside in the direction of their car. They passed an electrical substation with hazard and general construction signs erected outside.

'Why do you hate storms so much, Dadi?' asked Kal.

Dadi shook her head. 'No, no, Kal. I love storms. They are a message from Indra, the king of heaven, promising to lend his power to protect those who cry out for his help. This is all good. What I don't love so much is getting wet,' she concluded wisely.

As the family passed the substation they saw a workman outside. Dadi looked at him, concerned. 'Sir, you should be careful. An almighty thunderstorm is coming.'

The workman looked at the sky just at the moment they all heard a distant rumble of thunder. 'Thanks for the heads-up. You don't want to be anywhere near here if that substation gets hit by lightning. It'll take out the whole grid.'

Dru looked at the substation, an idea forming. He turned to the workman. 'Could you show us what you're doing? My brother would be really interested. He wants to become an electrical engineer.'

Dadi turned to Kal in surprise. 'Is this true?'

Kal wasn't sure what Dru was up to but knew he had to play along. 'Um, yes . . .'

Dadi looked thoughtful. 'Well, then. You'll need to study much harder.'

The workman shook his head. 'Sorry, I can't really let the public in.'

Now that Dadi realised this was an educational opportunity for her grandson, she was not going to take no for an answer. 'Oh, come on, sir. A quick peek for a budding electrical engineer?' Dadi flashed her winning smile.

The workman relented and let them in. 'Okay. But just for a second.' He stepped into the cramped substation, which was full of cables, switches and transformers. The twins joined him while Dadi stayed outside, looking up at the sky with a frown.

Inside, the workman pointed to some cables. 'Over there are some pretty standard high-voltage transmission lines.'

Kal shot a bewildered look to Dru but played along, nodding enthusiastically as Dru slipped away and looked around.

'Wow, that's amazing,' said Kal.

The workman was so delighted by Kal's interest he continued to talk nonstop. 'It all operates with a three-phase alternating current through a synchronised grid.'

'So interesting,' said Kal, looking as though he'd rather hang washing on the line than listen to this guy talk about electricity a moment longer.

While the workman continued educating Kal, Dru took a casual walk around the substation. He scanned the mass of cables and wires.

'The power runs into the substation at a trans-mission-level voltage, but then of course it's stepped down to distribution-level voltage so it can go out to the distribution wiring. Now, as I'm sure you will have ascertained, each service location on the grid has its own required service voltage.'

Dru grabbed a document labelled GRID SERVICE MANUAL and flicked quickly through it. There were instructions on the substation and a map of the facilities. Perfect! Dru hid the manual under his T-shirt and moved back out to join his brother near the entrance.

Another rumble of thunder sounded.

'Wow, that was all *so* interesting, but we have to go now,' said Dru as he quickly pulled his brother away.

Dadi smiled at the workman. 'Thank you so much. And don't forget the storm. It's on its way.'

CHAPTER TWO

Back in the white room at GCI headquarters, Rose and Mack, still wearing their white jumpsuits, lay on their beds, bored and restless. Mack's jaw was aching and he rubbed it, trying to soothe the pain.

A noise at the door made them look and turn. A security guard held the door open while Dr Sharma stepped in. She was carrying the tin.

'I'll be right outside if you need me, Dr Sharma.'

'Thank you. The examination shouldn't take long.'

The guard left the room.

Maya looked around the room, noting the position of the surveillance camera in the top left corner of the room. She smiled at Mack and Rose benignly. 'My nephews brought me too much lunch. I thought I'd share it with you.'

She placed the tiffin on the table by their beds. 'How are we feeling after the procedure yesterday?'

Rose just shrugged.

Mack answered quietly. 'It's a bit sore.'

Maya nodded in sympathy. She moved closer to him, and checked his jaw. Making sure the cameras couldn't catch her speaking, she whispered in his ear, 'Eat this as loudly as you can, okay?'

She opened the tiffin and placed it before him. Mack picked up a samosa and bit into it. 'Oh, yum, this is good. Mm. Mm.' He chewed and exclaimed loudly.

Maya then stepped over to examine Rose. She moved in closely. 'Is there a plan?' Rose asked quietly. Maya looked at Rose seriously. 'I'm working on it. Be ready.'

Mack handed a samosa to Rose and she took a bite. 'Wow, this really *is* tasty!' she said.

•

At the Sharma household, Dru lay on the floor of the twins' bedroom, reading through the pages of the service manual he'd taken from the electricity substation. They were complex, but this was the only plan they had for possibly breaking Rose out of GCI headquarters.

Kal sat at his desk, his desktop computer on, scrolling through his social media feed.

Dru turned a page. 'According to the service manual, if that substation goes down, the whole area around it will lose power, including GCI headquarters.'

Kal was less than enthusiastic. 'Okay. But for how long?'

Dru ignored his brother's lack of enthusiasm. 'Says here it takes six minutes for the emergency backup to kick in.'

'Six minutes isn't long,' said Kal. He looked at Dru's hopeful face. 'But it could be long enough, I guess.'

Dru smiled.

'So, how do we take down an electrical substation without getting caught . . . or electrocuted?' asked Kal.

'Don't worry, I've got an idea,' said Dru, flicking through the remaining pages of the manual. 'But we'd have to find a way to get inside the substation without anyone seeing us.' He found the map page and looked closely. 'There's an underground access point here,' he said, pointing to the map.

Kal wasn't thrilled. 'I don't want to go back into any tunnels, bro.'

The twins had worked out that the implant didn't work when Kal went underground. This should have been a good thing, but Dru knew it made Kal feel terrible. Kal had described the first time – when they had gone to visit the Unlisted in the tunnels – as feeling like he had received an electric shock, followed by nausea and weakness. He'd hated it and really wasn't keen to relive that memory again anytime soon, and Dru didn't want to make him.

'Then we'll need help,' he said pragmatically.

Before Kal could reply, a message from Regan popped up on his computer screen: 'Wanna hang out?'

Dru glanced over, annoyed. 'Why is Regan messaging you? Does she think you're her best friend now?'

'I dunno, Dru,' answered Kal defensively. 'She probably just wants to hang out.'

Dru wasn't happy with that answer and gave his brother a searching look. The last thing he wanted was some kind of alliance between Regan – their classmate and general busybody bully – and his brother. It was too dangerous.

At that moment, the computer lost power, the bedroom light flicked off and the rest of the house was plunged into darkness. 'Huh?' said Kal. 'What just happened?'

'Dadi,' said Dru with a knowing grin. Dadi was always concerned the house would get hit by lightning in an electrical storm, so she thought it best to turn off everything, much to the family's annoyance. But as they were well aware, once Dadi's mind was made up, it could not be unmade.

Dadi entered the boys' bedroom. 'Don't be scared, wombats. Just a precaution. You know Mrs Gosling at number thirty-seven lost her computer to a power surge in a storm only last month.' Dadi used the Mrs Gosling story every time, and every time it was only last month that Mrs Gosling had been the victim of a power surge. How was that possible? The answer was, it wasn't, unless Mrs Gosling was particularly unlucky with computers, but what could you do?

Dru scrambled to think of a reason to leave the house. He knew it would be hard to come up with a plausible excuse, but he had to. 'We should go next door and tell Chloe to do the same.'

Dadi was pleased by her grandson's suggestion. 'Yes, a very good idea, Dru. But don't stay outside for long with the storm coming.'

The boys headed downstairs and got on their bikes, bypassing Chloe's house altogether and heading towards the tunnels. 'Maybe Dadi will think we decided to stay and hang out with Chloe,' Dru said as they sped off.

•

Unfortunately, they didn't see Regan arrive a second later on her bike. She'd come around to see Kal and was disappointed to have missed him. But she saw the twins ride away, and decided it might be interesting to follow them. Although she was starting to trust Kal, especially after they'd spent the day hanging out at the Adrenoblast gaming centre, she didn't think Dru was taking his Elite status as part of the Global Child Initiative seriously enough. And frankly, he always seemed to be acting suspiciously. She pedalled after them, carefully keeping far enough back so that they didn't notice her following them.

When the boys arrived at the tunnel entrance, Dru went in to update the Unlisted on the substation plan, and Kal hid out of view nearby. He watched in confusion as Regan approached on her bike. She looked around and walked over to the boys' abandoned bikes. She quickly dropped her bike next to theirs, and entered the tunnel before Kal had a chance to stop her.

CHAPTER THREE

Inside the tunnels, Regan was tempted to turn around and head straight back out. The lighting was bad, the noise of scuttling creatures echoed, and it was damp and gross. But she was sure this was where the Sharma twins had gone, and her curiosity won out.

She continued a few steps further and then something happened. It was like a force field hit her. Her fingers started twitching, her legs buckled from under her and she felt completely drained of energy, like she'd just run a marathon. She collapsed against a rough concrete wall, frightened and unsure about what was happening. Then the weird feeling passed, but she still felt weak and nauseated.

Slowly, she moved away from the wall, and tested whether her legs could take her weight. She felt a pounding in her head. She still wanted to find the twins, but now it was because she wasn't sure what was happening to her and didn't want to be alone anymore.

She stumbled down a tunnel, hoping it wouldn't be long before she glimpsed a familiar face.

•

Dru had arrived at the Unlisted's hide-out, unaware that he had been followed. Kymara, Jacob and Gemma were pleased to see him. He knew without them telling him that without Rose there, they were feeling lost and helpless.

Dru explained what he had learnt from his aunt, Maya, earlier in the day: that Rose and Mack had tried to escape but had been caught; and that on top of the drones that were still searching for the

Unlisted kids, there was going to be a new army of Super Recognisers.

Jacob was alarmed. 'Unbelievable. So, now we have to worry about Super Recognisers too?'

Kymara shook her head, shocked at the lengths Infinity Group were willing to go to find the kids. 'How will we know who they are?' she asked.

Dru grimaced. 'We won't. Unless they're wearing uniforms, which they probably won't be. Bua said they're hiring hundreds of Super Recognisers, so they'll just look like normal people.'

Gemma had listened quietly to Dru's story, but now she spoke, and her determination was clear. 'I don't care how many drones or super whatevers there are – we have to help Rose! It's my fault she was caught, and Mack too. I'm the one who teed up the time for the meeting with Mack, and then –'

She stopped to take a breath and calm herself. Then she looked directly at Dru and said: 'I'll take my chances with those Super-Recogniser people. Just tell me how we're getting Rose out.'

Dru was grateful for Gemma's enthusiasm. He handed her the map from the service manual. 'I've marked it here. If you follow these access tunnels, you'll end up under a substation close to where Rose and Mack are being held captive,' he said. He was about to continue when he heard a clatter of cans nearby.

The kids sprang up, looking for a place to hide, but seconds later Regan appeared in the entrance to the hide-out. Dru's first reaction wasn't shock so much as concern – Regan looked terrible. He quickly realised that she must have suffered the same way Kal had underground, and she was obviously still battling dizziness and fatigue. She looked around the hide-out, eyes wide, and at Jacob, Kymara and Gemma. Her gaze landed on Dru and, even in her weakened state, she smirked. 'I knew you Sharmas were up to something. You're going down.'

'Regan, no,' started Dru, but he remained frozen, unsure about the best way to handle the situation.

Regan turned to go but stumbled over some litter.

When she went to stand again, Kal blocked her path. 'You're not going anywhere, Regan.'

She gasped, looking trapped and still weak.

Dru had never been so happy to see his brother. He could tell Kal was affected by being underground, just like Regan was, so he bolted over to help support his brother.

Dru grinned at Kal. 'Nice to see you, bro.'

'You're welcome,' said Kal.

'Why is she here? Clearly she's not one of us. What are we going to do with her?' asked Kymara.

The others looked at Regan.

Jacob sighed. 'She needs to stay in the hide-out for now. We can't let her go.'

Regan glared at him. 'You can't hold me against my will!'

Gemma's reply was equally fierce: 'You shouldn't have stuck your nose in where it doesn't belong.'

Regan eyed Gemma carefully, quieted by her outburst. 'Whatever,' she said eventually.

The Unlisted, along with Kal, left Regan in the corner, pale and sulking, and moved out of her earshot so Dru could outline his storm plan.

'We need to keep moving,' he finished as all the kids heard a rumble of thunder above.

A reluctant Kymara agreed to stay behind to guard Regan, while Jacob and Gemma headed down the tunnel, followed by Dru and Kal. When they heard a drone approaching, Jacob picked up a rock and threw it a distance away, down another tunnel, and the drone immediately flew in that direction. They started moving down the tunnel again, Dru helping the still-struggling Kal. Dru consulted the map and was about to lead them into a tunnel when another drone appeared.

They flattened themselves against an alcove as the drone got closer. 'I think it's coming back this way,' Dru whispered nervously.

Gemma picked up a lump of concrete and threw it as far as she could down a very narrow shaft. The drone took off after the noise, and smashed against the wall of the shaft. It was a small victory, but one each of the four teens felt. There was some high-fiving and it left the gang feeling more positive about what could be done in this David and Goliath fight.

Kal was looking sick and Dru knew he had to get his brother out of the tunnel system. He handed the map to Gemma and Jacob and showed them the way. After whispered goodbyes, he helped Kal to the closest exit and they emerged above ground.

Gemma and Jacob ventured deeper into the tunnel system.

CHAPTER FOUR

Kymara definitely picked the short straw: left behind to guard Regan while the others tried to save Rose and take out the substation. She sat, restless, blocking Regan's path. Kymara kept her cap pulled low, trying to obscure her face from Regan's intense stare.

Regan, pale and drained, did not look the slightest bit happy with the situation. 'Where are they going?'

Kymara kept her face turned away from Regan. 'None of your business.'

Regan stared hard at Kymara. 'I already saw your face. I know you're Kymara Russell – that gamer.'

Reluctantly, Kymara turned to face her prisoner. 'Guess we really do have to keep you here forever, then.'

Regan struggled to her feet. 'Not gonna happen. I'm out of here.' She tried to stagger out, but Kymara stood up and barred the doorway. 'You're not going anywhere,' she said. She shoved Regan's shoulder and Regan gave up, knowing she didn't have the energy to win. She moved back and sat, defeated. 'I'll be leaving as soon as I catch my breath.'

Kymara just shook her head.

The silence between the girls was interrupted by a crack of thunder. Soon heavy rain was pouring down into the recess behind them.

More out of boredom than interest, Kymara said, 'So, you have the implant. What does it feel like?'

Regan turned away to stare at the wall. 'I don't know what you're talking about.'

Kymara laughed. 'Don't you? Haven't you wondered about how different your life's been over the past couple of weeks?'

'What do you know about my life?' retorted Regan, still refusing to make eye contact.

'I know that you're being mind controlled, and that you're being treated like lab rats by some kind of organisation that's pretending to have kids' best interests at heart, but it really doesn't.'

'Mind controlled?' said Regan. 'I think you're spending too much time gaming and not enough time in the real world, Kymara.'

'So, you fainting in class and losing consciousness in a park while snooping on Kal and Dru is just run-of-the-mill Regan stuff, is it?'

Regan started to look a little uncomfortable. 'Things have certainly been a bit . . . different from normal,' she finally admitted.

Kymara looked around, taking in their surroundings. 'You're not the only one to feel like that,' she said wryly.

Despite the situation and their mutual distrust, the girls started to open up. Regan turned to look at Kymara and asked her some questions, but she claimed not to believe what she was being told. 'You're saying the Global Child Initiative is a front for something called Infinity Group?'

Kymara nodded.

Regan was clearly taken aback but continued, 'And you think they've implanted all of us?'

'That's pretty much it,' replied Kymara.

'To make us better at everything?' questioned Regan.

'Everything except thinking for yourselves. And – I guess – going into tunnels.'

Kymara sensed that deep down Regan knew what she was telling her was ringing true, but Regan just didn't want to believe it.

'Great story. One question. *Why* would they do any of that?'

Kymara shrugged. 'We don't know.'

Rain continued to pour down the back wall.

'Well, excuse me if I don't believe someone who's keeping me prisoner in a tunnel,' said Regan, defiant.

Kymara was now faintly amused by the girl's staunch attitude. 'Suit yourself.'

Regan crossed her arms and turned away from Kymara. Moments later she turned back, pointing to the water that had started to pour into the chamber where they were both sitting. 'Is *that* supposed to be happening?'

Kymara looked at the water. 'Oh. Um. No, that's not good.' She stood as the flow of water became heavier. 'That's *really* not good. Wait here. I'm going to check it out.' She ran out of the space, turning back briefly to see Regan looking terrified but trying not to show it.

•

Once above ground, Kal returned to his new-normal strong self, and the twins made their way back to the substation to wait for Gemma and Jacob. There was no sign of the workman from earlier, and the substation was locked. Kal looked up at the sky, dark with thick black clouds, ready to begin pouring rain any minute. 'Now what?'

'We wait,' Dru said decisively.

'Dadi should get a job as a weather presenter. She knows what she's talking about,' said Kal.

Dru rolled his eyes. 'You mean she should be a meteorologist.'

'Same difference,' said Kal with a shrug.

Luckily they didn't have to wait long: the door to the substation was wrenched open from the inside by Gemma just as the rain started to fall.

Gemma and Jacob had followed the map Dru had given them and found a manhole at the top of a ladder exactly where he'd pointed out the substation was. It had been hard to move the cover off but the two of them, each balancing on the rung of the ladder, had been able to push it to the side.

After climbing up into the substation, the two Unlisted teens wasted no time. Gemma rushed to the main door.

'Good timing,' said Kal in greeting, as the twins moved inside out of the rain.

Dru was all business. 'Okay, good. So, once the substation goes down, GCI headquarters will lose power for six minutes. All main functions will be out: doors, CCTV, tracking systems.'

Kal held up a stopwatch.

Gemma was ready to move. 'What are we waiting for?'

Dru held his hand up, gesturing for her to stop. 'You and Jacob need to stay here. There are Super Recognisers everywhere.'

Gemma wasn't happy. 'We can't just do nothing!' A huge flash of lightning illuminated the doorway, accompanied soon after by a booming crack of thunder.

'You won't be doing nothing,' explained Dru. 'This substation is about to be struck by lightning.'

Gemma looked at Dru. 'What are you talking about?'

Kal grinned. 'We need you to be the lightning.'

Gemma and Jacob now both looked really confused. Rolling thunder announced that the storm was picking up speed. Dru quickly showed them the main power source, and how to switch all the circuits on.

'Are we going to get electrocuted?' asked Jacob, clearly worried.

'Not unless the substation actually does get struck by lightning,' said Dru.

Gemma looked panicked. 'So, it's a possibility?' she asked.

'You'd have to be really unlucky,' said Dru with an apologetic smile.

'I *am* really unlucky,' said Gemma, eyes wide.

Jacob gave her a pat on the back, trying to hold back a smile. 'We've got this, Gemms.'

Kal nodded. 'And as soon as the power goes out, you should head back into the tunnel system. You'll be fine.'

Jacob nodded but didn't look convinced.

'We have to go,' said Dru, and the twins ran out into the rain.

CHAPTER FIVE

Dru and Kal stood outside GCI headquarters, hoods up, lurking behind cars in the car park. Dru lifted his walkie-talkie to his ear. 'All good, Gemma?'

There was a crackle from the walkie-talkie. 'Yep, ready for the surge,' answered Gemma.

A flash of lightning accompanied another boom of thunder and Gemma yelled, 'Now!'

Dru and Kal saw the streetlights surge for a second before going off completely, leaving only the backdrop of the dark sky. The office building they were watching also went dark. Operation Storm Surge had worked.

Kal pressed time on the stopwatch. 'Six minutes,' he said.

The boys looked at each other and then made a dash into the building.

Inside GCI headquarters, all was dark. The metal detector had no power, the glass doors were open and security staff were evacuating a steady flow of employees out into the car park.

Dru and Kal managed to sneak in unnoticed. They watched from their position crouched behind the huge reception desk as their aunt appeared and walked down the stairs into the foyer, where she was approached by a security guard. 'Please head outside, Dr Sharma. All staff are assembling in the car park.'

Maya spotted her nephews but didn't look happy to see them. She seemed resigned, though, as if she knew she didn't have a chance of stopping them. She drew the security guard closer to her. 'Okay,' she said loudly enough for the twins to hear. 'But first, can you help me with something?' The guard looked at her impatiently but she smiled politely and continued as if she hadn't noticed his reaction. 'My pass hasn't been working properly. Could you take a look at it?' She did her best to position herself so that the guard had to turn away from where the boys were hiding, to face her.

The twins ran behind their aunt and the guard and across the foyer. They had almost made it to safety when another guard looked up. 'Hey, you!' he yelled.

Dru and Kal bolted into the gloomy interior of a stairwell as a security guard gave chase. 'Pursuing intruders through Stairwell B,' the guard yelled into his earpiece as he grabbed a torch and ran after the twins.

•

In the white room, Rose and Mack were sitting on the floor when they were plunged into darkness.

After a moment of silence Mack said, 'Is this a trap?'

They waited a few moments in case Emma Ainsworth appeared, but nothing happened.

Rose felt a glimmer of hope. 'It's too quiet,' she said. She wasn't going to pass up the opportunity of potentially getting out of there. She stood up, and pulled Mack to his feet. This time they didn't have a pass to open the door, but if there was no power . . . she pushed the metal doors to the room – and they opened. 'The electronic security system's been disabled,' she said to Mack. 'Something must have gone really wrong.'

Mack and Rose crept out into the darkened corridor. Hurried footsteps could be heard from the far end. A torch beam skimmed the floor near the runaways as two security guards approached from the corridor that led to the white room.

Rose and Mack narrowly escaped being seen as they ducked behind a metal cabinet in the hallway next to the entrance of their room. The two guards rushed into the room, and in one swift movement Mack pushed the heavy cabinet so it toppled in front of the door, blocking the guards' exit.

Mack stopped and regarded himself with surprise. 'I never could've done that before.'

'Let's keep going,' said Rose.

They raced down the corridor and heard more footsteps approaching. Rose frantically tried a couple

of doors and found an open one, and pulled Mack
into the room, shutting the door behind them.

•

'What is *that*?' Kal hissed as they saw an overturned
metal cabinet blocking a doorway. 'Isn't that where
Rose and Mack should be?'

Amid the sound of fists banging against the door,
the twins heard adult voices calling, 'Is anyone there?
Let us out!'

'Looks like they got away!' Dru said. 'Let's go.'
He led the way back down the corridor and around
a corner and was turning to confer with Kal about
which path to take when suddenly an arm reached
out and pulled them both into a room.

Dru switched on a torch and shined a light – right
into Rose's face. *Sh*, she indicated with a raised finger
to her lips before they could speak.

Another guard raced past towards the sounds of
the trapped guards banging on the door. Once the
sounds of the footsteps had faded away, Rose and the
twins shared a hug.

'I'm so glad to see you,' said Rose. 'And this is Mack,' she added.

'Hi,' the twins said hurriedly.

'Oh, you're identical twins,' said Mack, looking between the two of them, surprised.

Kal looked at his stopwatch. 'Two minutes nineteen seconds,' he said to his brother, pointedly.

Rose grinned. 'You caused the blackout?' she asked, impressed.

Dru shrugged humbly. 'Figured it was the best way to get you out of here,' he said.

'Nice!' said Rose.

'Two minutes thirteen seconds until the power kicks back in,' said Kal. 'We need to move.'

Rose nodded and headed out the door and to the right, but the twins stopped her. 'No, we can't go that way. They're assembling in the car park. We need to go left.'

Kal took the lead, leaving the others no choice but to follow.

•

Back at the tunnels, heavy rain continued to pour through the ceiling grate and into the chamber. Kymara returned to the hide-out, drenched to the bone.

Regan was still sitting on the floor, looking scared. 'What's happening?' she asked.

Kymara rushed past Regan and started moving junk, uncovering an old ladder lying underneath. 'Help me move this ladder!' she yelled.

Regan stayed still. 'Why?'

Kymara glared at her. 'Because the tunnels are flooded and the water's rising!'

Regan, still weak, stood up sulkily and helped Kymara uncover the ladder and together they moved it over to the grate.

Kymara pointed up. 'That's our only way out, unless you'd like to try swimming through the tunnels back to the entrance?'

Regan shook her head.

'Okay then. Feel free to help if you want to stay alive,' said Kymara. She climbed up the ladder and, trying to protect her face from the pelting rain, reached up to open the grate. 'Argh!' she shouted. 'It's padlocked shut!'

Regan looked up expectantly as Kymara calculated her next move. She hurried down the ladder and reached out to a perplexed Regan.

'Don't touch me!' said Regan defensively, reaching up to slap away Kymara's approaching hand.

But Kymara ignored her and grabbed a metal hairclip from Regan's hair with a tense smile, then climbed back up the ladder. At the top, still battling the heavy rain, she inserted the hairclip into the padlock.

An increasingly stressed out Regan paced beneath her, wading in ankle-deep water. 'Do you even know what you're doing?'

Kymara stabbed at the lock, frustrated and without success. She removed the clip, momentarily defeated. Wiping water from her eyes, she refocused and inserted the clip into the lock once more, this time taking greater care to not jam it in. This time, it worked. The padlock released, and with the palm of her hand Kymara banged at the grill until it popped open.

As she tried to pull herself up to the ground above, the ladder wobbled in the water, threatening to tip over.

Kymara yelled over the sound of the rain. 'I need you to hold the ladder steady while I pull myself out!'

'No way!' Regan replied, sounding panicked. 'You'll leave me here. I'm gonna go first.'

Kymara was steadfast. 'You can't. You're too weak. I'll pull you up. I promise.'

Regan stood, frozen at the bottom of the wavering ladder. The rain kept pouring in and the water level was rising.

Kymara tried again, through gritted teeth. 'We don't have time to argue. Trust me.'

A reluctant Regan had no choice. She steadied the ladder as Kymara pulled herself up and out of the small opening. First her head, then her torso, and finally her feet disappeared from view.

Regan was alone in the hide-out, looking up at the grate entrance, getting soaked by the water. 'Hello? Don't leave me here!' Regan looked around her at the water rising. Was she really going to have to swim to safety?

Then Kymara's face appeared above the grate, followed by one arm. 'Start climbing, Regan. And hurry, I'm lying in a puddle here!'

Regan carefully took a couple of steps up the ladder, and took hold of Kymara's arm.

CHAPTER SIX

Kal, Dru, Rose and Mack reached the empty goods entrance, and were able to leave the building through a fire exit, undetected.

Mack pushed a large skip in front of the door, blocking it. He looked to the others and shrugged. 'It worked in our favour last time.'

The rain had lessened, and the storm had almost passed, but they still kept their heads down and ran as quickly as they could to the perimeter of the car park.

Kal consulted his stopwatch. 'Time.'

The lights to the building flickered and turned back on. Alarms shrieked in the distance. Nobody noticed the four escaping teenagers as they ducked behind cars, shielding themselves from view.

Rose saw a leather-clad courier making his way towards his scooter, and she made a snap decision. She lifted up his back pannier and slipped something from her pocket into the container. Moments later, the courier arrived at his scooter, started the engine and drove off. Rose returned to the others, who looked at her quizzically.

'What was that?' asked Dru.

'Your aunt was supposed to implant me, but she slipped it under my tongue instead.' Rose grinned as the scooter disappeared into the distance. 'That should lead them on a wild goose chase. Let's get out of here.'

The three boys laughed, but then Mack looked concerned. 'I can't go with you. I have an implant. They can track me.'

Rose nodded. 'I'm not leaving you behind, Mack. Come with us.' She smiled warmly. 'We'll think of something. Right?'

Dru and Kal shared a glance that showed that neither of them was sure what that something might be.

Security guards were now moving out of the building, spreading out in what appeared to be the beginning of a search. Dru knew the longer they waited, the more likely they were to get caught. 'We have to go.'

Mack suddenly turned and ran away from Rose, Dru and Kal, and towards the guards. 'Run! Now!' he yelled back to them.

'Mack! No!' shouted Rose.

But Mack ignored her. 'I'm over here. Come and get me!' he yelled to the guards.

In his stark white jumpsuit he attracted attention easily, and the security guards immediately raced over to Mack, while the other three made their escape.

Dru, Kal and Rose ran around the back of the GCI headquarters. They kept running and were racing up to the substation a minute or two later when a figure jumped out to stop them.

'Rose!' shouted Gemma in delight, engulfing her friend in a hug. 'It's so good to see you.'

Jacob quickly followed and hugged Rose too. 'Good to have you back, buddy,' he said with a grin.

'It's so good to see you both,' said Rose, feeling teary.

Gemma looked at the twins. 'Where's Mack? Did you find him too?'

Kal tried to explain. 'We did, but –'

'But what?' asked Gemma. 'Where is he?'

Rose sighed. 'They implanted him yesterday, Gemms. And he didn't want to come with us because they could have tracked him, which would have put us all in danger.'

'I don't understand,' said Gemma, clearly upset. 'Where did he go?'

'He stayed behind at headquarters,' Rose said quietly.

Gemma looked broken.

'Well,' said Jacob with forced brightness, 'it's great you made it, Rose.' He gave Gemma a pointed look.

'Of course it is,' said Gemma. 'It's just . . .'

Rose gave Gemma another hug. 'I know.'

Dru turned to Jacob. 'Why didn't you go back down the tunnel underneath the substation?'

Jacob frowned. 'The tunnels were flooded. The flash-flooding must have hit the drainage system really hard.'

'But . . .' The implication hit the others. 'What about Kymara and Regan?'

Nothing more needed to be said. The five teens ran towards the tunnels as fast as they could.

•

Barriers had already been put in place blocking the entrance to the tunnels. The teens hid in the bushes and overheard a council worker speaking on his mobile. 'Yeah, it's Neville from Council. The whole underground network's flooded to the brim. Mate, it'll take days to drain out!'

The five teens looked at each other in shock. What did that mean for Kymara and Regan?

They watched the council worker leave the area, and were crouched, silent, when a very damp

Kymara pounced on them from behind. 'Hey! Why the long faces?' she said with a laugh, giving Rose a hug. 'About time you came back,' she said. 'Did you miss us?'

'Of course,' said Rose. 'But how did you get out?' she asked, pointing to the tunnel entrance.

Kymara smiled smugly. 'I could ask you the same thing.'

Rose looked at the girl now standing behind Kymara. 'You're Regan, right?'

'And you are?' she responded defiantly.

Rose snorted. 'As if I'm going to tell you anything. You'll just run back and tell Infinity Group.'

'No, I won't,' said Regan.

The twins scoffed. 'No-one's going to believe that, Regan,' said Dru. 'You'll do anything to remain an Elite.'

'You're wrong,' said Regan. 'Now I know the truth. Kymara told me. They've implanted us without our consent. Over the past couple of weeks I've noticed I can do all these new things.'

'Yeah. And you've loved every minute of it,' said Kal.

'Maybe some of it, but it's not worth it if I don't have control over my own brain,' said Regan.

'Got it,' said Kymara as she stopped recording on her phone and her hands flew over the keypad. 'Uploaded to a secure site.'

Regan groaned.

'I've put it behind a password-protected security wall,' Kymara added.

Rose stood tall and stared at Regan. 'If you make any trouble for us, it goes straight to the Global Child Initiative.'

'Your Elite status won't help you then,' Kal threw in.

'You'll end up like Jiao,' added Jacob.

'And Mack,' said Gemma quietly.

'Fine,' said Regan, looking equal parts annoyed and exhausted. 'I get it.' She stalked off, without a backwards glance.

The remaining teens – Dru, Kal, Rose, Gemma, Kymara and Jacob – turned back to face the entrance to the tunnels. It was starting to get dark, and they needed a new home.

'So, what now?' asked Jacob. 'Where do we go?'

There were no easy answers to that question. But Dru simply smiled.

'You're coming home with us,' he said.

Kal nodded. 'Yeah, why not.'

The Unlisted looked incredulous.

Half an hour later Rose, Gemma, Jacob and Kymara were inside the garage at the Sharmas' house. The twins had smuggled down pillows and sleeping-bags, as well as biscuits from the pantry, while Dadi, oblivious, watched her favourite reality TV program in the lounge room. The group looked settled, dry and happy to all be together again.

'Thanks, you two,' said Kymara on behalf of all four of the Unlisted. 'We owe you.'

'No problem,' said Kal.

Dru and Kal quietly pulled down the aluminium garage door. 'Not sure how long this is going to remain no problem,' said Dru quietly to his brother.

At that moment Dadi came out onto the balcony and called to the boys. 'Wombats? Are you out here?'

The boys ducked down, out of Dadi's sight.

She listened for a moment longer, and then sighed, moving back inside.

The twins shared a look. That was close. Too close.

CHAPTER SEVEN

Early the next morning, the four Unlisted kids lay
on the ground in the Sharmas' back garden, with the
sun on their faces.

'Oh man. This feels so good,' said Gemma.

'Right?' agreed Jacob.

'Your garage wasn't the most comfortable place I've
ever slept,' said Kymara to Kal and Dru, who were
standing nearby, 'but it was much, much better than
sleeping in a tunnel!'

The Sharma twins were both in school uniform.
They watched their new friends enjoy their freedom,

but they were all nervous about being out in the open, with Super Recognisers – and everyone else, it seemed – on the lookout for 'missing' kids.

Kal looked up the street and saw his parents' car coming down the hill. 'Quick! Mum and Dad are back from the gym. Back in the garage.'

'Go, go, go!' said Dru.

The Unlisted ran back into the garage. The twins shut the roller door after them, and a second later Rahul and Anousha pulled into the driveway. They got out of the car wearing their workout clothes, surprised to see the twins standing around in the driveway. 'Why are you boys up and out so early?' asked their father. 'Is the house on fire?'

'We're just doing some morning yoga,' Kal replied quickly.

'Since when have you been into yoga?' asked Anousha, with a confused smile. 'Have aliens taken over my sons?'

Dru spluttered, 'Uh . . . you inspired us.'

Rahul raised an eyebrow and looked at Anousha. 'How do you like that, Noush? We're inspiring!' He beamed with pleasure and the two of them walked into the house, sharing a laugh.

•

It was not easy to organise breakfast for the Unlisted under the watchful eye of Dadi. As the TV in the corner played a morning current-affairs program, Kal and Dru collected as many cereal boxes as they could, and were trying to figure out how to sneak out some milk when Rahul came downstairs, freshly showered and beaming at his sons. 'You know, if we cleared out that garage,' said Rahul. 'I bet we could use it as a family yoga room. We could get started straightaway.'

'No!' shouted Dru.

'No!' echoed Kal.

'The garage is full of spiders,' said a panicked Dru.

The blood immediately drained from Rahul's face.

It was well known in the Sharma family – and the greater neighbourhood – that their father hated spiders and would avoid them at all costs.

Kal threw his brother an appreciative glance.

'Oh, who needs the garage, eh,' said a shaken Rahul. 'We can do yoga in the living room.'

Dadi appeared and immediately noticed the boys with their stockpile of cereal. 'Why all this sugary cereal, boys?' she asked indignantly. 'Vidya has her big assessment today – she needs a nutritious breakfast.'

'Oh, okay. In that case, could you make *upma* then, Dadi?' asked Kal. The thick porridge made from dry roasted semolina was a Sharma family favourite.

Dru backed him up 'Like, lots and lots of upma?' Dru was sure the Unlisted would love Dadi's food. Everyone did.

Dadi didn't take much persuading. 'Good idea. We shall have a mountain of upma!'

As Dadi set about opening cupboards and chatting to herself about ingredients, the news item on the TV caught the twins' attention. In the background, an image of a substation appeared behind a newsreader.

'. . . the Minister for Energy was quick to respond to yesterday's blackout, stating that the power outage was fixed in record time, with mobile phone coverage being restored almost immediately.'

Emma Ainsworth appeared onscreen, seated in the TV studio. Beside her was Mack, glassy-eyed and unhappy-looking, sitting next to a smiling man.

Dru and Kal exchanged a worried look.

'Could we turn this up?' asked Dru.

Onscreen, the newsreader continued her bulletin. 'Thirteen-year-old James McNamara was reunited with his father, Don, after being found by members of a special Global Child Initiative task force dedicated to locating missing youth. James and Don join us in the studio, along with Global Child Initiative Chair, Emma Ainsworth. Welcome, all of you. This is certainly a good-news story.'

Mack's face was blank, in stark contrast to his overjoyed father.

Dismay registered on Dru's face at the sight of the altered Mack.

'It really *is* a good-news story,' smiled Emma to the interviewer. 'We're thrilled to have played a part in this family reunion. While James is not yet a hundred per cent, we're sure he will make a full recovery under the care of his father and with the help of the GCI.'

'What has the community response been to your Child Location Program?' asked the interviewer.

'It's been a joy to see the public engage with what we're doing,' answered Emma. 'And we're ramping up our efforts before the Global Child Congress this week.' Emma turned to the camera and addressed viewers. 'If anyone at home would like to help our displaced and disadvantaged youth –'

But the rest of the call-out remained silent as the screen turned black. 'Let's keep moving, Sharmas,' Anousha said as she put down the remote.

'I was watching that!' said a disgruntled Dadi. 'Now I don't know how to help our disadvantaged youth.'

Anousha rolled her eyes at her melodramatic mother-in-law.

Kal squeezed his eyes closed, grimacing – clearly he was in a lot of pain.

Dru watched his brother with concern. He asked quietly, 'Are you okay?'

Kal replied sharply, 'I'm fine. Back off.'

Dru was shocked, but refrained from replying.

Vidya had come in halfway through the TV report, and was now busy eating breakfast. 'Is it just me, or does that Global Child Congress thing sound kind of creepy?'

Dru and Kal focused on their food, but Dadi immediately disagreed with her granddaughter. 'I like that they're helping youngsters. It breaks my heart to see children homeless and without food.'

Rahul smiled appreciatively. 'You should give those kids some of your upma, Mum. That'd sort them out,' he joked.

Dadi looked at her son. 'It's not such a bad idea. Maybe I should borrow Kavya's son-in-law's food truck.'

Anousha looked at her mother-in-law and shook her head. 'I don't think he meant you should actually –'

'Oh yes,' Dadi continued as if Anousha hadn't spoken. 'Oh yes. It is worth thinking about.'

CHAPTER EIGHT

Kal and Dru managed to sneak down to the garage before school with Dadi's special breakfast, which the Unlisted ate appreciatively straight out of the saucepan.

'It's delicious,' said Jacob with a satisfied scrape along the bottom of the pot.

Dru and Kal told the gang about seeing the subdued Mack on TV, which quickly evaporated the joy of eating a hot breakfast.

'Poor Mack,' said Rose. 'When I was at headquarters I overheard Emma Ainsworth talking about the Global Child Congress – I'm pretty sure that's the day they talked about making the mind control permanent.'

Kymara looked shocked. 'Permanent? Not gonna lie. That sounds bad.'

Kal looked miserable.

'Dru, you might be able to do something with this.' Rose handed him a USB. 'I stole it from an office at headquarters on our first escape attempt. It might have information that can help us stop what's going on.'

Dru looked it over closely. 'Well, it's worth a try. Thanks, Rose,' he said, turning the key over in his hands.

Kal looked at the key in his brother's hand and reached out to take it. 'It's okay, I'll hold on to it.'

But Dru didn't loosen his grip. 'No. I'll take it to school. If it gets us on the system, maybe we can work out how to disable the implants before it's too late.' He pocketed the key as he stood, trying to ignore Kal's glare.

Dru turned to the Unlisted. 'We need to get to school now. Mum and Dad are at work, and our sister's at school. Dadi will be home until ten this morning but then she'll go to the market. So, after she's gone you'll have the house to yourself for about an hour.'

The kids' faces lit up.

'Oh my gosh, that means I can take a shower,' said Gemma.

'We'll leave the side door open for you,' said Kal. 'But be careful.'

'And make sure you're back in here before Dadi gets back. If she sees you, we're all toast,' said Dru.

•

At Westbrook High a group of students wearing yellow ties painted a yellow border around a small section of the playground. Regan stood in front of the crowd. 'Trace the borders properly,' she instructed.

Kal and Dru entered the school grounds, relieved to have arrived before the morning bell. Tim stood by the school gate, handing out flyers to every student who passed. 'Help find these missing children today.'

It was bizarre for them to see what had happened to their school in such a short amount of time. The yard used to be filled with kids hanging out and joking and taking it easy; now everyone in their class wore colour-coded uniforms and performed chores without complaint but also without enjoyment. And Tim – the old Tim, before he'd been taken away – would never have handed out flyers helping the government or the school faculty. He'd have been kicking a ball on the football field, or telling dumb jokes, getting to class late with his shirt untucked and his shoes covered in mud.

Kal and Dru took a flyer each and noticed photos of each of their four friends among a host of other 'missing' children. Kal nudged Dru and they both looked over to Regan, unsure whether to trust her. She now knew almost as much as they did about GCI, and she could ruin everything if she decided to turn them in.

'Morning, Sharmas,' she said with her usual smirk.

The twins looked at her cautiously.

She stared back at them, giving nothing away.

Chloe walked up the path between the twins. She seemed anxious, which was understandable; school had turned into a battleground for Basics. 'Help find these missing children today,' said Tim robotically.

Chloe absently took the flyer and kept walking, trying not to attract attention.

But Regan stopped her. 'Chloe, why aren't you wearing your tie?'

Chloe looked down, and panicked. 'Please don't report me, Regan. I forgot it. I can just run home and get it. Please.'

Regan looked at Kal and Dru, then back to Chloe, and said quietly, 'I never saw you.'

'Thank you! Thank you!' said Chloe and she ran back out of the school gate.

Some of the kids tasked with painting the yellow borders had paused and were looking at Regan curiously. She turned to yell at Dru and Kal. 'What are you two looking at? Get to class!'

The twins didn't have to be told twice. Awkwardly carrying the flyers Tim had given them, they headed quickly inside.

•

As soon as ten o'clock arrived, the Sharmas' garage door opened a crack. Rose and Jacob lay on the concrete floor and peered out at the driveway, checking to see if the coast was clear.

From inside, Gemma asked, 'Has she gone?'

Rose nodded. 'I think so.'

Gemma crawled out under the garage door first, but froze at the sound of footsteps.

She turned back to Rose, panicked.

'Come back! Quickly.' Rose gestured for her to return to the safety of the garage.

Gemma slid back under the door, and Rose pulled it shut behind her.

They waited in the darkness, hardly daring to breathe.

Two sets of footsteps approached the front door, and then the doorbell rang.

'Hello?' said a soft, accented voice.

One of the strangers replied. 'Good morning, ma'am. We're representatives of the Global Child Initiative.'

The Unlisted all froze, straining to hear more and trying not to make a sound.

'Oh,' the soft voice said, 'are you collecting money for charity? To help find all those lost children? I'll just get my purse.'

The GCI woman answered, 'That won't be necessary, ma'am. We're going door to door asking residents if they can keep a lookout for these displaced children. Here, if you could just take a copy of this flyer? And if you see them –'

But the soft voice didn't let the loud one finish. 'I should bring them home and give them a good meal,' she said enthusiastically.

'No, ma'am,' said the GCI representative. 'We ask that you do not speak to them directly. Frightened children can sometimes act in unpredictable ways. If you do see any of them, please notify us immediately.'

The Unlisted listened to the silence for a moment, then heard a gentle reply. 'Okay then. Will do.'

Gemma, Kymara, Rose and Jacob held their collective breath as the double footsteps receded, and a minute later they peeked out to see the twins' grandmother leave the house, pulling her shopping trolley behind her as she headed to the local market.

CHAPTER **NINE**

As soon as the boys' dadi disappeared out of sight, the Unlisted escaped from the garage and went around the side of the house, where Kal had left the door unlocked.

Quietly and carefully, they opened the external kitchen door and stepped into the house. Apart from Gemma and Kymara's visit to Mae a few days earlier, this was the first time they had been in a real house in weeks.

Gemma wasted no time. She went to the pantry and found a big jar of Nutella. Delighted, they all dipped spoons in, scooped some out and '*Yum*-ed' and '*Ah*-ed' happily at the chocolatey goodness.

Kymara slipped out of the room to explore the rest of the house as Jacob turned on the radio in the kitchen and was delighted to hear hip-hop being played. 'Real music! Remember that?' Jacob, Rose and Gemma danced along to the song.

Kymara discovered Vidya's bedroom. On her dressing table, she looked at perfumes, make-up and deodorant. Kymara tried everything, spraying perfume onto her old clothes. She clocked Vidya's theatrical make-up along with a few prostheses and a couple of latex masks.

Gemma and Rose entered Vidya's room and instantly coughed. 'I think you went a little overboard with the fragrance, Kymara,' said Rose with a smile. Kymara responded with an extra spray of the perfume in the girls' direction.

'Ugh. We're suffocating here,' said Gemma with a giggle.

Gemma wandered over to the dressing table. 'This

is Dru and Kal's sister's room, right? What's up with the freaky masks?'

'Maybe a school assignment,' suggested Rose, taking a look at them.

Kymara was impressed. 'She's really good, don't you think?'

Jacob went upstairs, where he found Kal and Dru's bedroom. He wandered through the room, sat and bounced on the beds, thinking longingly of his own. He inspected Kal's posters, and then took a close look at the twin's trophy collection. Dru was a chess champion, while Kal's trophies were all related to football. Jacob smiled. He bumped one of the trophies and it almost fell, but he righted it and heard a rattle in it. Curious, he peered inside – and recognised the item. It was the crystal USB that Rose had given Dru earlier, in the garage. Dru had been adamant he wanted to keep hold of it – so, why was it hiding in one of Kal's trophies? Jacob felt uneasy. Something wasn't right. Making a quick decision, he dashed to the boys' wardrobe and grabbed a hoodie and a pair of sunglasses.

Without telling the girls what he was doing, he ran down the stairs as quietly as he could, grabbed a skateboard he'd noticed up against the side of the house, and skated off down the road.

•

Dru and Kal were sitting in the back row as Mr Cunningham addressed the class. He pointed to the whiteboard, which contained a complicated maths equation. 'Solve the following equation . . . and no talking, please. The point of the exercise is to have you answer these questions on your own.' He glared at the students.

Dru was now aware he had to look as brainy as everyone else in the class, which was getting harder and harder as the strain of everything he knew about Infinity Group and GCI clouded his mind. He blinked and took another look at the board, before glancing out the window . . . where he saw Jacob pop into view for a moment.

What? He looked around the class, scared someone else had seen him, but most of the class was concentrating on the equation – except for Regan, who slowly glanced out the window, and then back towards Dru, with a raised eyebrow.

Dru started to sweat. He still couldn't tell whether Regan was friend or foe. He stared again at Jacob as if to say, *Are you crazy?!* But Jacob stayed where he was. He obviously wanted Dru to come out to him, and wasn't going to budge, despite the obvious danger.

An announcement came over the school PA system. 'Mr Cunningham, can you please move your car? You've parked the principal in.'

Mr Cunningham sighed in undisguised annoyance. He fumbled in his pockets for his car keys then turned to Regan. 'Regan, you're in charge. I'll be back in a minute.'

Regan nodded eagerly. 'Of course, Mr Cunningham.'

Dru saw his opportunity. 'Sir? Can I please go to the bathroom?'

Mr Cunningham absent-mindedly agreed. 'Okay. Go ahead.'

Dru quickly left the classroom and ran around the side of the building, where Jacob was waiting for him.

Checking that nobody could see them, Dru launched in. 'What are you doing here? If they catch you, they'll –'

Dru stopped talking when he saw Jacob pull the USB out of his pocket.

Jacob handed it to Dru. 'You said this morning you need to test this on the school system,' said Jacob.

Dru was surprised. 'How did you get that? I thought it was in my pocket.'

Jacob gave Dru a serious look. 'I was just taking a look around your bedroom, and I almost knocked over one of Kal's trophies. It was *inside* the trophy,' explained Jacob.

'Thanks for bringing it in,' Dru said, confused and a little worried. 'Were the girls okay with you coming here?' he asked.

Jacob gave a cheeky smile. 'I better head back.'

The two boys heard footsteps approaching. 'Be safe,' whispered Dru as Jacob pulled up his hood, put the sunglasses back on and skated off.

•

Chloe had taken much longer than she'd meant to at home. Her yellow tie had been washed by her mother, but then had gone missing in the washing pile. She'd finally found the annoying bit of material partially hiding under the washing machine after searching her room three times. Which meant she was really late for school. She was trying to work out what excuse might work to stop her from getting in more trouble, when she spotted a teenage boy cruising past on a skateboard. She instinctively took a photo of him with her phone. What was a kid her age doing skating instead of being in school anyway? She hated her next thought but she couldn't stop it: Might this be a way to get back in the good books with the Global Child Initiative?

As Chloe entered the school grounds she saw Mr Cunningham walking away from his car. She rushed to catch up with him. 'Excuse me, Mr Cunningham. Can I show you something?' she asked excitedly.

Mr Cunningham was agitated. 'You're late, Chloe. Go straight to class.'

Chloe persisted, hoping the teacher would be pleased with her news. 'It's about those missing children, sir.'

Mr Cunningham stopped and looked at her. 'Go on,' he said.

She shoved her phone under his nose. 'Look. I saw him up the street.'

Mr Cunningham studied the image. 'Did you see where he went?'

Chloe shook her head 'He took off on his skateboard.'

Mr Cunningham smiled at her. 'This is extremely valuable information, Chloe. You will be rewarded for this.' He quickly attached the photo to a text message and sent it to his own phone before handing the phone back to Chloe.

This was exactly what she wanted to hear. All of a sudden her tie being stuck under the washing machine was the best thing that had happened to her for days. 'I will? But I'm just a Basic,' she said.

'Not for long,' replied Mr Cunningham with a smile. 'Now, off to class.'

Chloe grinned to herself as she skipped into school.

CHAPTER **TEN**

Dru decided he might as well actually use the school bathrooms considering that had been his excuse for leaving class, and by the time he returned to the classroom, the bell had just rung. The students streamed out, and Dru fought against the tide to pack up his things. Regan stayed behind and watched him, and when the last student had left the class, she closed the door behind them. 'What was your friend doing here?' she asked. 'If he got caught, he'd bring us all down with him.'

Dru stared at her. '*Us?*'

'Well, yeah. We're in this together now. Aren't we?' she asked, looking a little vulnerable.

Dru looked to the desk, where Mr Cunningham's laptop lay open. 'Well, keep guard at the door for me then,' he said, before taking out the USB and plugging it into Mr Cunningham's laptop.

Regan was fascinated 'What are you doing?'

'I think this USB is kind of like a key,' Dru explained as the screen sprang to life with the words: INFINITY GROUP: ACCESS ALL AREAS.

'Bingo. We're on the system,' said Dru. 'And no alarms, because it's all legit.'

Regan forgot standing guard at the door and stared over Dru's shoulder, fascinated, as Dru navigated Infinity's network. He clicked on a link labelled 'Infinity Group Investor Report', and a video started to play onscreen: Emma Ainsworth, seated at her desk looking down the barrel of the camera. 'Hello, investors and stakeholders,' she said, every inch the corporate professional, 'and greetings from Infinity Group headquarters. Our environment is changing – heatwaves, tsunamis and rising temperatures – but I'm happy to say that your position as a world-class leader is secure. This year has brought solid results from our Global Child Initiative. Next year we will expand to ten new countries, and in five years we will roll out our first generation of behaviour-regulated workers and enforcers – compliant and at your disposal.'

Dru was horrified. He froze the video. 'This is so much worse than we thought,' he muttered, so concerned he didn't notice Regan clutch her head in pain. He removed the USB, pocketed it and the screen went blank.

Regan stood with her head in her hands.

'Are you feeling all right?' asked Dru.

She winced and replied, 'No, not really. I've been having these really intense headaches.' They heard footsteps in the corridor and sprang away from Mr Cunningham's laptop a moment before the door opened and the teacher entered.

He saw Dru and Regan busily tidying chairs into lines. 'Don't worry about that. Off to your next class,' he barked gruffly.

Dru and Regan collected their things and made their way out of the room, their hearts beating loud and fast.

•

Back at the Sharma house, Gemma lay on the lounge listening to the music from the radio in the kitchen, grateful for a moment of relaxation.

That moment was ended abruptly by Rose. 'Do you know where Jacob is?'

Gemma shrugged. 'No. Wasn't he having a shower?'

At that moment Kymara entered wearing Vidya's bathrobe and a towel around her head. 'Nah, it was me in the shower,' said Kymara.

Suddenly the sound of keys in the front door made them all freeze. Then Gemma almost fell off the couch in fright. 'She's back already?!' she cried.

They all ran, scattering in different directions. From her spot behind the curtains, Gemma watched the woman Dru and Kal called 'Dadi' enter the kitchen, oblivious to the panic she had created. She had a whole lot of groceries in her shopping trolley, which she had started to unpack onto the bench when she stopped, head raised with a look of confusion on her face.

The radio!

Gemma silently groaned as the pop music blared from the radio.

'Such rubbish,' she muttered, and went to move the dial to another station. Gemma almost sighed in relief – until she saw Dadi run her finger over the radio dial and then hold it up to her nose.

No, the Nutella!

Dadi seemed confused but shrugged it off. After wiping the radio with a cloth, Dadi found the frequency for an Indian-influenced station, and Gemma stifled a panicked giggle as Bollywood music blared from the speakers. Gemma watched Dadi put the last of the groceries away, all the time wondering how she and her fellow Unlisted would make their escape, when she and Dadi both froze.

There was a distinct thump from upstairs. It was barely audible over the music but Dadi's attention was piqued.

Gemma held her breath as she watched Dadi move slowly out of the kitchen.

●

Kymara lay as still as possible, doing her best to impersonate a sleeping teenage girl beneath a theatrical prosthetic mask – something she never imagined she would have to do. She heard a knock on the bedroom door. 'Emu? Are you home already?'

The door opened, and Kymara heard a soft laugh. 'There you are,' said Dru and Kal's grandmother. 'So sneaky in your fantastic mask. How did your assessment go this morning?'

Kymara knew she had no hope of sounding like Vidya – she had never met her – so she simply put her thumbs up in the air and hoped for the best.

Dadi seemed satisfied with the response. 'Well done. You must be exhausted. Rest, rest.' She closed the door, and Kymara almost fainted in relief.

●

Rose had heard Dadi move towards Vidya's bedroom and thought she had enough time to slip out the kitchen door and sneak back into the garage. Unfortunately, just as she went to open the door, Jacob opened it from the outside. Rose got the fright of her life and had to stifle a scream. When she'd calmed down, she was angry. 'Where have you been?!' she hissed.

'I found the USB you gave Dru this morning hidden in the boys' room,' he replied, matching her whispered tone. 'I think Kal had taken it from Dru.'

Rose stared at him. 'Kal? But what if someone saw you!'

The tense conversation was cut short as a high-pitched scream came from the kitchen. Rose and Jacob whipped around to see Dadi staring at them, wide-eyed. 'Burglars! I'm calling the police!'

Rose tried to calm the old lady down. 'Wait. Please, Dadi – don't call the police.'

Dadi looked at her indignantly. 'I am *not* your dadi.' She grabbed her phone and punched in numbers. 'Hello? Police? I'd like to report two –'

It was then that Gemma and Kymara appeared in the kitchen, eliciting another scream from Dadi. 'Four! Four youths in my house!'

But her fear was replaced by narrowed eyes. 'Actually, never mind,' she said and ended the call. The four confused teenagers watched as she pulled a flyer off the fridge. She squinted at the images on the flyer, looking closely from it to each of them.

Kymara tried to calm Dadi. 'We're friends of Dru and Kal.'

'We need your help,' said Jacob plaintively.

Dadi didn't respond. She dialled the number printed on the flyer and looked over at the Unlisted. 'I know how to help you.' They watched her wait for the call to be answered, and they all froze as they heard her next words. 'Hello? Global Child? I had a lovely man and woman visit me today and –'

Kymara was the first to spring into action. She turned the volume up on the radio to its maximum setting.

'What's that?' Dadi shouted into the phone. 'Speak up. I can't hear you!'

While all this was going on Vidya walked in from the front door to find Dadi yelling into the phone, loud music playing and four teenagers she'd never seen before in her life, in her kitchen. Even worse, one of them was wearing her dressing gown.

'Dadiji! What's happening here?' She looked around at the Unlisted. 'And who are *you*?' she yelled over the music.

Dadi hung up the phone in frustration.

Kymara turned the radio off. 'Please, hear us out. If you decide to turn us in then, you can.'

Vidya and Dadi looked at each other and then the kids. Dadi gripped the phone in her hand a little tighter.

CHAPTER ELEVEN

Finally, the school day came to an end and students filed out into the afternoon sunshine.

Dru watched Kal grimace as he put on his helmet at the bike racks. 'Another headache?' he asked.

'I'm fine,' Kal responded sharply.

Dru threw his own helmet on the ground and rounded on his brother. 'How are we supposed to work together if you keep lying to me?' he snapped.

'I told you at lunch, I didn't steal the USB,' said Kal, fighting back. 'I thought it would be safer if it was kept hidden.'

Dru was about to make a sarcastic retort when Kal jumped on his bike and rode off without him.

Of course Kal beat him home – Dru had no hope against Kal's enhanced speed – but he at least waited for Dru in the driveway after dumping his bike. The boys still weren't speaking to one another, though, as they walked into the kitchen.

They both froze in the doorway when they saw Gemma, Rose, Jacob and Kymara sitting with Vidya and Dadi, finishing off what looked like a mountain of freshly cooked food. Their friends looked showered and were dressed in various items of clothing pilfered from the twins' and Vidya's wardrobes.

Dadi turned to her grandsons. 'Hello, wombats. Is there something you forgot to tell me?'

The twins looked at each other, speechless. But then they took a seat and caught up on what the Unlisted had already told Dadi and Vidya.

'This is a lot to take in, children,' Dadi said. 'I can't believe I fell for this Global Child rubbish. I even asked Aunty about that food truck! All your other aunties wanted to help.'

'How many aunties do you have?' asked a confused Gemma.

Kal laughed. 'Everyone's an aunty.'

Jacob nodded in agreement. 'That's what it's like with my family friends as well. I feel ya,' he said with a grin.

Maya arrived a moment later and called the boys aside. 'We have to get them out of here – now.'

Dadi hugged her daughter. 'The children told me everything. I'm so glad you're okay,' she said.

Maya turned to the boys. 'You told your dadi?' she said angrily.

The twins shrugged. 'Not exactly,' said Dru.

Maya gritted her teeth. 'Jacob was sighted in the area today and a report went back to headquarters. There will be Super Recognisers sweeping the neighbourhood. We have to get you all out of here immediately.'

The doorbell rang and everyone froze – except Dadi, who mobilised with the speed of a woman half her age. She rushed towards the hallway and saw that the two Global Child staff who visited earlier were again at the front door. 'Maya, take them to the garage,' said Dadi to her daughter, motioning to the Unlisted. She turned to the twins and Vidya. 'You kids stay here.'

The two Super Recognisers impatiently rang the doorbell again.

Dadi, thinking quickly, threw on a dressing gown, wrapped a towel on her head, and opened the door.

'Good afternoon, ma'am.'

Dadi poked her head around the door. 'I'm sorry. I've just drawn myself a bath. I'm an old lady. I have sore joints. It's not a good time. You'll have to come back.'

The Super Recognisers did not look pleased. 'We're doing a second sweep of the neighbourhood.' She showed Dadi the picture of Jacob. 'This child has been spotted in the area. Have you seen him?'

Dadi shook her head. 'Poor boy. I hope you find him. Goodbye.' She closed the front door quickly, leaving the Super Recognisers unimpressed but unable to push the issue any further.

•

In the garage, Maya waited with the Unlisted. Gemma paced, agitated. 'What's taking them so long?' she asked.

'We just have to wait a little longer,' reassured Maya. 'They'll come for us when it's safe.'

Suddenly the roller door opened. Dadi, Vidya and the twins stood in the driveway. Behind them was an old Volkswagen Kombi van; on the side was a painted sign that said 'Breakfast at Tiffins'.

It was quite a sight. The Unlisted giggled as they saw Dadi looking very pleased with herself. 'Your chariot awaits,' she said with a twinkle in her eye.

•

The food truck weaved through traffic, Bollywood music blaring from the speakers, until it arrived at a cinema in the eastern part of the city. Dadi pulled to a stop, and the back door to the cinema swung open. Amir, a middle-aged Indian–Australian man, stepped out. He wore colourful seventies clothing and an excited smile.

'*Jaldi. Jaldi.* Quick!' he yelled to Dadi and the kids.

The Unlisted and Maya ran from the food truck and into the cinema.

Dadi gave Amir a big hug. 'Amir. Thank you, old friend.'

He smiled. 'They'll be safe here.'

Amir gestured to the kids to move further inside the cinema. 'Any friends of the Sharma family are friends of mine. Please make yourselves at home. Butter popcorn and choc-tops for everyone.'

The kids were enchanted by their new surroundings. On the drive over Dadi had told them proudly that her friend Amir owned the old Indian cinema, and had painstakingly renovated it, keeping it open as audiences became smaller and smaller. Now it only opened during special Indian festivals or Bollywood nights. So, it was the perfect hiding place for four teenagers who didn't want to be found.

The auditorium had comfortable velvet chairs, and when Amir waved up at the projector room, the projector cranked into life. A classic Bollywood film started to play on the screen. It was a surreal moment for the Unlisted: within twenty-four hours they had gone from a waterlogged tunnel to a suburban garage and now they felt like royalty watching movies in a cinema open only for them. They were all aware things hadn't really changed, but they could certainly enjoy the moment. Kymara and Rose tapped popcorn boxes. 'Cheers, big ears,' said Kymara with a laugh.

Jacob and Gemma were already halfway through their choc-tops, grinning as they watched the poor but impossibly beautiful Indian girl dream of a better life than the one she had cleaning toilets in the majestic Rajasthani palace.

CHAPTER TWELVE

Kal sat at his desk doing homework while Dru rummaged around, opening and closing drawers, rustling under bedclothes, getting more and more worked up.

Their father knocked and entered the room. 'Do you know where your dadi is? Food's nearly ready. It's not like her to miss dinner.'

Vidya, passing by the room, answered before either of the twins had to come up with a lie. 'She's with Mooni Aunty. They're out in the food truck feeding the homeless. I'm sure she'll be back soon.'

'Well, I suppose that's a good excuse,' said Rahul.
'Have you finished your homework, Kal?'

Kal paused for a moment and then replied, '*Hahn
Papaji. Main sabse buddhimaan hoon. Main sabse takatwar
hoo.*' In English this meant, 'Yes, Dad. I am the
smartest. I am the strongest.'

Rahul looked at his son with immense pride. 'Your
Hindi is really improving, *beta. Bahut aacha.*' He headed
back downstairs, and Dru rolled his eyes at his brother
before diving back into his search. 'I can't find the
USB anywhere. Are you sure you don't have it?'

'Not this again,' Kal replied in annoyance. 'I told
you I don't have it!'

Dru sat on his bed and thought for a moment.
'Maybe I dropped it in the garage.' He left the room
and went to look.

Kal pulled the USB out of his pocket and smiled.
In Hindi he said, '*Antim ulti gainti shuru hoti hai,*' which
translated to 'Begin final countdown.'

•

Dru was up early the next morning while Kal slept, still obsessing over the missing USB. He searched again, checking every place he had checked the previous night, hoping it might magically appear – but, nothing.

Having thoroughly searched his side of the room, Dru pondered his brother's half. He quietly moved over to Kal's side and started looking through his brother's belongings. Suddenly Kal's hand shot out from under his doona and grabbed Dru's arm, his eyes remaining closed.

'Three thousand, one hundred and twenty minutes until mission complete,' said Kal robotically.

Dru was shocked. 'What?!'

Kal blinked his eyes open. 'You right there?' he asked in a cranky voice.

'What just happened?' asked Dru.

'Uh, I woke up. With you in my face,' answered Kal.

'No – but . . . you grabbed my arm. And then you said something weird.'

'Yeah, sure I did,' said Kal sardonically as he sat up in bed. 'Feel free to go back to your side of the room, brother.'

'I need to find that USB. It gets us on the GCI system. That means it could bring down the mainframe at headquarters, or give us remote access to the network and –'

'Okay, okay,' Kal said sleepily, holding up a hand. 'I haven't seen it, but good luck. It's too early for your stress.'

'I'm stressed because we have two days until the Global Child Congress. Or "three thousand, one hundred and twenty minutes", right?'

'What are you even talking about?' Kal asked, rolling himself out of bed and heading for the bathroom.

As soon as Kal stepped into the hallway Dru looked through his belongings, shifting bedclothes, searching his bookshelf and around his desk. When he moved a framed photograph, the USB fell out from behind the frame.

Dru picked it up, shaking his head. This was the second time Kal had stolen the USB from Dru – and lied about it. It felt like Kal was losing more and more control over his actions. And it also felt like Dru was losing his brother.

•

'Come on, emu, roll like you mean it,' said Dadi encouragingly as Dru entered the kitchen.

Vidya groaned. 'I'm going as fast as I can.'

Dru looked at the piles of chapatis Dadi and Vidya had already made to go with the Tupperware containers of food. He was about to ask when the food would be delivered to the Unlisted, but Anousha and Rahul arrived, ready for work, and Dru knew to keep his mouth shut.

'Nice to see you helping your dadi,' said Rahul, giving his daughter a kiss on the forehead.

Vidya looked uncharacteristically nervous. 'I – um – we . . . Dadi said I need good karma! That's the only reason I'm helping.'

Anousha frowned. 'Why are you being so defensive?'

'I'm not!' said Vidya defensively.

Kal came rushing in, inadvertently saving Vidya from putting her foot further in her mouth.

'Smells epic!' He went to open one of the boxes of food.

'Thank you, Kal,' said Dadi, flattered. 'But stop right there. It's not for you.'

Anousha and Rahul watched, confused as Dadi swatted him away.

Kal stepped in and whispered to Dadi, 'Where are you taking all this stuff?'

Dru knew that now was the time for him to step in. 'Time for school, Kal,' he said, pulling his brother towards the door. 'Gotta go.'

He threw a forced smile at his parents as he dragged Kal outside.

'What's the rush?' said Kal.

'Oh, you know. Mr Cunningham doesn't like Elites to be late,' said Dru as they put on their helmets and biked down the road.

At the first intersection they stopped at the sight of a huge billboard boasting a GCI poster. The slogan:

INVESTING IN THE CHILDREN IS INVESTING IN THE

FUTURE was written in large block letters. The poster featured images of all the 'missing' kids – including Kymara, Jacob, Rose and Gemma.

Dru read the slogan aloud, then added: 'I guess you could call permanent mind control an *investment*.'

Kal gestured to the faces on the billboard. 'I still don't know where Dadi's hiding the others. Has she got them at a friends' house or something?'

Dru looked uncomfortable. 'Uh . . . something like that. I haven't heard exactly.'

Kal shot Dru a suspicious look. 'Oh, okay. Cool.'

Dru returned the look. 'You're totally sure you haven't seen that USB. Right?'

'Yeah, man. I'll let you know if I do.'

'Okay. Cool,' said Dru.

They eyed each other for a moment before riding off.

•

Melodious Bollywood music filled the cinema as the credits rolled in front of Rose, Kymara, Jacob and Gemma. Pillows, blankets and sleeping-bags lay around the theatre.

'What just happened?' asked Rose.

'I'm not sure, but I liked it,' answered Gemma, wiping away tears. 'It was romantic.'

Jacob shrugged. 'The dancing was good.'

Amir appeared, invigorated at having a new audience for his Bollywood film collection. 'Did you enjoy that one? Of course you did! The dance numbers went gangbusters all over the world.'

Kymara raised an eyebrow. 'You mean they went viral?'

'Sure. Viral. Okay,' said Amir, his enthusiasm undimmed. 'Who's ready for another? More popcorn for all!'

'Or how about some real food?' said Dadi, who appeared at the top of the stairs, laden with containers.

Within minutes everyone was ripping lids off the Tupperware.

Jacob shoved a whole chapati in his mouth. 'Dadi, you are amazing.'

'Stop it,' she said mock-bashfully. 'Actually, keep going. You are right, of course.'

Jacob hiccupped. And again. He tried to keep eating, but his hiccups continued.

'Slow down,' said Gemma. 'You'll choke.'

Jacob answered by hiccupping again.

Dadi gave him a warm smile. 'Don't worry, hiccups are actually a very good omen. In India, we believe it's a sign that someone is thinking of you.'

Jacob hiccupped.

'You're lucky, Jacob,' said Rose.

'How exactly?!' he said between hiccups. 'I can't even eat.'

'At least someone's thinking of you,' she said sadly. 'My parents think I'm gone. I can't believe I might not be there when my baby brother or sister is born.'

'Don't worry, little koala,' said Dadi gently. 'You'll be back with them before you know it.'

Rose stood up and moved away from the rest of the group.

Dadi and Amir shared a look of concern.

CHAPTER THIRTEEN

The twins approached the school gates where Chloe stood, looking wary. 'Hi. Am I allowed to talk to you, or . . .'

'Um, yeah, sure,' said Dru, but Kal was less kind. 'She's a *Basic*, Dru.'

Dru felt Kal's eyes on him. He looked up to see Regan on the other side of the quadrangle, also watching.

'Sorry, Chloe,' said Dru. 'Regan's watching us. You know how she is.'

Kal walked off, and Chloe looked over at Regan. 'Yeah, I know. It's okay. I have a feeling things are about to change, though.'

'What do you mean?' asked Dru, anxious. He really didn't think he could cope with any more change!

Chloe gave Dru a confident smile. 'You'll find out soon enough.'

Dru was perplexed by Chloe's attitude, but he knew he had to keep up appearances, so he ran to catch up with his brother.

Once in the classroom, the students found their seats. The moment Mr Cunningham walked into the class, he tapped his tablet. The students' eyes glazed over and they stood up, chanting, 'Three thousand and fifty minutes until mission complete.'

Dru imitated his classmates while quietly freaking out.

Mr Cunningham nodded and ticked something off on his tablet, which as far as Dru could tell prompted the students to return to their normal state while remaining standing.

'Good morning, class. In preparation for the Global Child Congress, Basics and Cores will spend today completing drills while our Elites go to headquarters for the final step in their training. Elites, to the front of the class. The rest of you can sit down.'

The class sat as Kal headed to the front of the room. Dru, Tim and Regan joined him. Suddenly, Chloe stood too.

'What's she doing?' Dru asked Kal quietly.

'Chloe has been very helpful in our missing-child search,' said Mr Cunningham. 'As a reward, she has been promoted to Elite status.'

Mr Cunningham passed Chloe an Elite tie and she handed over her Basic one, thrilled to have received the upgrade. She put on her tie and immediately looked more confident. She moved to the front of the class. 'According to Global Child Initiative rules, I get to choose whose spot I'm going to take.'

Mr Cunningham nodded in agreement. 'There can only be four of you from this year group.'

There was shock from the four Elites.

Chloe walked past each Elite slowly, enjoying the revenge. She looked at Tim and kept moving. She stopped at Dru. 'Please remember who your friends are, Dru.'

She moved past Dru to Kal.

Kal held her eye, refusing to cower.

'Kal. You've been pretty mean to me since you became an Elite.'

'Just doing my job,' said Kal coldly.

Chloe walked past Kal and stopped in front of Regan. There was a moment's silence before Chloe chirped loudly and clearly, 'Bye Regan.'

'What?!' said Regan, furious.

'You've had this coming for a long time,' said Chloe spitefully.

'But . . . I'm Year Leader!' She turned to Mr Cunningham, waiting for him to reverse Chloe's obvious mistake.

'Regan. Don't make this harder than it has to be,' he said instead.

'It's not fair!' Regan cried out in full tantrum mode.

'That's enough. For everyone else, tomorrow is a pupil-free day to prepare for the Congress; but Regan will be on in-school detention.'

He ordered Regan back to her seat and then said to the class, 'Your Elites will lead you to the quadrangle.'

Mr Cunningham eyeballed Regan grimly. With no choice, Regan returned to her chair, glaring at the other Elites as they marched out of the class. The Basics and Cores followed and then moved into formation in the quadrangle while Mr Cunningham observed.

All the while Dru watched Regan closely. It was clear she was already hating life as a Basic.

'Very good. Elites, come with me now, please,' ordered Mr Cunningham. He started walking away and three of the Elites followed him. As Dru reluctantly headed after them, Regan's hand grabbed his elbow.

'What?' said Dru.

'Listen. You have to be careful of Kal,' said Regan quietly.

This set alarm bells ringing with Dru. 'What do you mean?'

'I've been blacking out for the last twenty-four hours since the headaches started. Doing things and then not remembering them. They must be turning up the strength of the implants. And if Kal's got two . . .' she trailed off, her meaning crystal clear.

Kal looked back at Dru and frowned when he saw him talking to Regan. He jerked his head in a 'hurry up' motion. Dru quickly moved away from Regan, towards the Elites. 'Thanks, Regan,' he said quietly, hoping she heard him.

She nodded as she watched the Elites go, fear clear on her face.

•

Amir had put on an upbeat Bollywood musical to lighten the mood in the cinema. There was a bit of dancing, helped along by Dadi and Amir doing some choreographed moves, which the other Unlisted were attempting to follow with much hilarity. All except Rose, who was sitting alone. Gemma gestured to Kymara, and they both moved over to their friend. Gemma took Rose's hand as the girls watched the movie.

'You can't give up on us now,' said Gemma.

Rose sobbed. 'You didn't see my mum's face when they thought I might be . . . I wish I could let them know I'm okay.'

'Hey, Rose – you're the strong one, remember?' said Kymara.

Rose continued to cry silent tears. Gemma and Kymara didn't know what to do to make her feel better. They completely understood her sadness.

Dadi came over and sat next to Rose. 'Come here, koala.' She took Rose's face in her hands, looked at her and gave her a big hug. 'You *will* get through this.'

Dadi reached out a hand to Kymara and Gemma too. 'We'll all get through this, okay?'

Jacob sat down behind them. 'Hey, don't forget about me!'

Dadi reached out and included Jacob in the group hug. 'How could I forget this one?' she said.

Then, out of nowhere, the Bollywood music stopped and the cinema screen went blank.

'What happened?' asked Dadi.

Amir didn't look worried. 'It must be my satellite. The connection drops out sometimes.'

Kymara was instantly interested. 'Did you say satellite?'

'Yes. I have a receiver and a transmission relay. I get all the channels from India . . . I'm totally up to date with the soapies, and of course my Indian legends in the Indian Premier League.'

Dadi groaned. 'Please don't get Amir started on cricket.'

'No, it's cool. I want to hear more. It's giving me an idea.'

The walkie-talkie that Rose had been carrying in her pocket crackled to life. 'Come in. Are you there? Come in?'

Rose answered it. 'Dru? Is everything okay?'

'They're taking us to Global Child Initiative headquarters right now.'

The other Unlisted and Dadi crowded around Rose. 'Okay,' said Rose.

'This time there's only four of us going, only the

Elites, so I'm totally exposed. But I've got the USB . . . I'm gonna see if I can use it to take them down. Today.'

Dadi yelled at the walkie-talkie. 'Go wombat! You and Kal have got this!'

Dru's voice sounded less enthusiastic. 'Yeah . . . I don't know about Kal.'

'You can always rely on him. He's your twin. Your greatest connection on this planet.'

Dru continued. 'I need you guys to tell Bua I'm coming. See if she can help me get access to the HQ mainframe.'

'Okay,' said Rose. 'We're on it.' Her earlier sadness had evaporated. She seemed much happier now that she had a focus.

Kymara took the walkie-talkie from Rose. 'Hey Dru. If you manage to bring down their system, keep one video channel open. Then send us the satellite frequency.'

'Wait, what?' said Dru, not sure he'd heard right.

Kymara shot a look over at Amir. 'We're going to send a message to Infinity Group. Telling them *exactly* who beat them.'

Rose looked at Kymara, mystified. 'We can do that?'

Kymara nodded. Rose smiled and said to Dru over the walkie-talkie: 'I want our voices to be the first thing they hear when they realise they've lost!'

'Okay . . . let's hope I make it that far,' said Dru on the other end of the walkie-talkie. 'I've got to go.'

Rose said quickly, 'Remember – you're doing this for Unlisted kids everywhere.'

Dru gave a chuckle. 'No pressure, then.'

Dadi yelled out to her grandson, 'Be brave!' before the crackle of the walkie-talkie signalled the converstaion had ended.

CHAPTER FOURTEEN

Mr Cunningham led the Elites into the foyer of the GCI building. Tim and Chloe passed through the metal detector first, followed by Kal and Dru; Dru stuck to Kal's side so they wouldn't be scanned separately.

Suddenly Kal, Chloe and Tim stopped in the middle of the foyer and chanted, 'Two thousand eight hundred and fifty minutes until mission complete.'

Luckily no-one paid much attention to the identical twin who was a beat behind the other three Elites.

Emma Ainsworth, looking authoritative and completely in control, marched over to them, followed by a man in a lab coat and Dr Maya Sharma. 'You're here. Excellent.'

'Oh, you're –' started Kal but was interrupted by Emma.

'Emma Ainsworth. Yes, Kalpen, I am.' She turned to Mr Cunningham. 'You can go now.'

Mr Cunningham nodded obediently and stepped away from the group, looking a little starstruck to be in the presence of Emma Ainsworth. Dru would have found it funny if he wasn't so terrified.

'I want to congratulate you all on the impeccable leadership skills you have demonstrated,' said Emma.

'Thank you,' said the Elites in unison.

'You will be integral in making the Global Child Congress a success,' she continued.

Dru glanced towards Maya, who was standing slightly behind Emma. She pulled a small piece of paper from the pocket of her lab coat and held it up surreptitiously so only Dru could read it: *MAINFRAME ROOM, 1 p.m.*

'For what's coming next, you'll need internal strength and emotional resilience,' said Emma. 'And that's what we'll be testing today.'

As Maya slipped the note back in her pocket Kal turned his attention to his aunt, his eyes narrowing slightly. Emma, noticing that Kal's attention had shifted, also glanced towards Maya, who smiled innocently.

'Kalpen,' asked Emma pointedly, 'is there something you'd like to share with the rest of us?'

There was a tense moment as Dru watched Kal nervously. Was he going to rat Dru and his aunt out?

'Nothing, Ms Ainsworth,' said Kal.

Emma nodded, satisfied. 'Very well. Then let's get started.'

Dru breathed a sigh of relief. Kal seemed to be battling for control over his own mind, but his brother was still in there somewhere.

The Elites were taken to a control room, where footage of war played out. Soldiers were falling in the battlefield from gunshot wounds and it felt horribly hyper-realistic. Dru was flinching but Kal watched the footage with ease.

'How can you watch this?' whispered Dru.

Kal looked confused by the question. 'Why wouldn't I watch it?'

'This footage has been specially designed to elicit fear, sympathy and disgust,' explained Emma dispassionately. 'Be strong. Do not give in to those base impulses.'

Dru turned to see Chloe and Tim also looking squeamish.

Emma spoke to the woman in the lab coat as she observed the children's reactions. 'Continue to decrease empathy, Dr Smythe. And turn up compliance. Five points higher than we did this morning.'

Dr Smythe nodded and changed some settings on the tablet she was holding. Dru watched as Chloe and Tim immediately became more visibly relaxed, more comfortable with the material they were watching. Just like Kal.

Dru was still repulsed by what he was seeing onscreen but he did everything he could to keep his face neutral, as though he wasn't affected by the unending images of death and destruction.

'That's it,' said Emma, giving them a pep talk. 'Don't let yourself be weighed down by petty compassion.'

Dru glanced at his watch: it was almost one o'clock. 'Excuse me, Ms Ainsworth,' he said. 'Could I please go to the bathroom?'

Emma looked over at Dr Smythe, confused. 'What's that about?'

'Uh – his bladder must be full.'

'No, I mean. Is it normal?' asked Emma.

Dr Smythe nodded. 'Yes. The children will function as usual until we flick the switch at the Congress. Then all activities will be synchronised.'

'Fine, Drupad. You have two minutes. Don't dawdle.'

Dru nodded, relieved to be leaving this experiment behind. He resisted the urge to sprint out the door, and instead he walked slowly to the exit. The other three Elites didn't even notice him leaving.

•

At the cinema the plan was underway as Kymara pulled a dusty old video camera from a box and set it up.

Jacob sorted through a mess of cables at his feet and Dadi helped him untangle them.

Rose was seated with a pen and paper, drafting a message as Amir plugged two red coaxial cables into the back of the satellite receiver in his office.

Kymara switched on the camera and the video screen lit up. Gemma switched on the spotlight illuminating a single empty chair sitting in front of the camera.

Amir hurried up to the projection room and plugged a cable into the back of the satellite receiver.

Rose was in front of the camera, in the spotlight, while Kymara stood behind it. She looked pleased. 'We're ready to transmit as soon as we hear from Dru,' Kymara said with satisfaction.

Dadi was watching from the auditorium. 'Wait. Just wait a second. You can't let them see who you are.'

Rose disagreed. 'I *want* them to see my face.'

Dadi shook her head. 'Trust me, Rose. I've seen enough Indian soap operas to know that the secret villain is always the scariest.' She turned to Amir. 'Can't you pixelate her or something?'

Amir gestured to his old dilapidated camera. 'I bought this camera back in the nineties. How high-tech do you think it is?'

Dadi sighed. 'Fine. I'll take care of it. Like everything else.' She picked up Amir's large black hoodie from one of the seats and put it on Rose. The hood flopped over her head, obscuring her face. Under the spotlight, she looked imposing and sinister – and, most importantly, anonymous.

Jacob was impressed. 'Dadi, you really are amazing.'

Dadi looked over at Jacob. 'It's true, young man. And remember, you can never tell me too many times.'

Everyone cracked up at Dadi's ego, breaking the tension in the room.

•

At GCI headquarters, Dru loitered in an empty corridor, USB in one hand and walkie-talkie in the other. He knew he was taking a huge risk with all the surveillance cameras in the building, but he'd tried to find a corner of the corridor that was unseen by the cameras. He whispered into the walkie-talkie, 'Rose, I'm about to introduce a malicious subroutine into the mainframe. Be ready to transmit.'

The walkie-talkie crackled too loudly in reply, the noise echoing down the empty corridor. 'Ready when you are, over.'

Lowering the walkie-talkie, Dru moved towards the door of the mainframe. Maya appeared around the corner and threw him her pass and then continued down the corridor as though nothing out of the ordinary had happened.

Dru reached the door and swiped Maya's pass. The door unlocked and he entered the mainframe room. Inside he found a huge bank of cables, wires and switches. Taking the USB from his pocket, he found a spot among the forest of wires to plug it in.

Then he stepped up to a computer terminal. Typing quickly, he brought up a screen that read: WEDGE ACTIVATED FOR REMOTE ACCESS. KEY 94AXPQ9R.

Dru took note of the key, then navigated around pages of back-end code. He began typing a subroutine. 'Come on . . . got to get in before . . .' he pressed ENTER moments before a red window popped up, saying: SECTION LOCKDOWN.

'Yes!' said Dru. All was going to plan. Around him, various screens started flashing and shimmering, as though there was a problem with the electricity cabling.

On a nearby terminal, Dru brought up the satellite software system. He selected a button that said: VIDEO OVERRIDE. A number of frequency coordinates appeared on the screen. He pulled out his walkie-talkie. 'We're good to go,' he said calmly. 'Satellite code is one-one-zero-five-nine-capital H-two-three-seven-zero-zero.'

The crackle of the walkie-talkie responded. Rose's voice sounded triumphant. 'Dru, you legend! Kymara's typing the code in now . . .'

Over the walkie-talkie Dru could hear Kymara saying, 'Ready to transmit in three . . . two . . . one . . .'

Dru held his breath.

CHAPTER FIFTEEN

Chaos broke out at GCI headquarters. Security and laboratory technicians were running around panicking, trying to figure out where the message was being broadcast from.

Every screen in the building had been overtaken, and the image of a shadowy hooded figure appeared on every monitor, tablet and phone. Her message was forthright and fearless: 'We are the Unlisted. We are coming. You cannot control us. You cannot hold us back. You are not the future. *We* are the future.'

Warning lights flashed as security systems reacted to being hacked but were unable to find the source. The message began again: 'We are the Unlisted. We are coming. You cannot control us. You cannot hold us back. You are not the future. *We* are the future.' And again, on a loop.

Emma Ainsworth was trying to hold her frustration in check but was losing the battle quickly. In the testing room where Tim, Chloe and Kal had been watching the distressing material, Rose's image was now plastered on the screens, confusing the Elites. Was this part of the assessment too?

'What is going on, Dr Smythe?' Emma growled to the lab technician, her polished voice becoming lower and more menacing.

The technician tinkered on her tablet, looking nervous. 'It looks like someone's broken into the mainframe and . . . oh, this is surprising.'

'*What* is surprising?' snapped Emma.

'The break-in came from inside the building.'

Emma looked ready to explode. 'Put the building

in lockdown. Make sure no-one comes or goes. We have to find whoever did this.'

Chloe had stopped looking at the screen and turned to Emma. 'Ms Ainsworth? Dru Sharma's still not back from the bathroom.' She looked proud of her observation.

Kal was rattled. His brain felt like it was battling for control.

'Dr Smythe,' Emma said, her voice quiet and dangerous. 'Turn off that annoying video. And find Drupad Sharma.'

•

Dru ran down a corridor and peered into the foyer below, where screens continued to play the Unlisted message. 'Go Rose!' he whispered.

But the video of Rose disappeared from screens, and was replaced by the GCI logo. They'd managed to block the transmission, for now.

He turned left and almost slammed into a security guard. 'Hey!' he said. 'Come here!'

Dru ducked in through an unmarked door and ran for his life.

•

Back in the testing room Dr Smythe checked her tablet with a frown. 'The tracker says Drupad Sharma is right here. In this room.'

Emma was frustrated by the woman's stupidity. 'Well, clearly he's not!' She turned to Kal. 'Where's your brother?'

Kal hesitated.

Emma glared at him. 'You wouldn't want to lose your Elite status, would you?'

Kal blinked a couple of times before answering. 'I don't . . . I don't know.'

Emma was losing her cool. 'It definitely says he's in this room?' She gestured at the tablet. 'Give me that.'

Dr Smythe handed over the tablet. Emma moved over to Chloe and scanned her. There was a positive beep. Emma moved over to scan Tim. A similar beep. Then she moved to Kal, about to do the same thing. He instinctively stepped away from the tablet.

Emma's eyes narrowed. 'Stand still,' she barked. She scanned Kal. A tense moment, then there was a beep, followed a second later by a second beep.

Emma stared at the screen. 'How can . . .' She looked at Kal, then at the technician. 'Kalpen Sharma has two implants.'

Chloe gasped.

Kal looked terrified.

Emma pressed a button on the wall and two security guards entered moments later. She nodded towards Kal. 'Take him for further testing,' she said. 'And bring me Drupad Sharma. Now!'

•

Dru got to the end of the corridor and looked around, unsure where to go next. He took a sharp left and headed towards a fire-exit sign. But the security guard was gaining on him. 'You!' he shouted. 'Stop!'

There was no way Dru would get to the exit before the guard caught up with him. But then Maya appeared from a concealed doorway and blocked the guard.

'Get out of here!' she yelled to her nephew.

Dru hesitated, worried about his aunt.

'Go!' she said again. And he realised she was sacrificing herself for him, and he ran through the fire exit and out the door, tears streaming down his face.

•

There were celebrations afoot at the cinema. The Unlisted knew the broadcast had happened, and for the first time in what seemed like a lifetime they had revealed themselves at a time of their choosing. And they had been fierce. So fierce.

'I can't believe it! I can't believe we just did that,' said Rose. 'We're awesome!'

'We took them down!' said Jacob

'And rubbed it in their faces!' said Kymara.

'We're the Unlisted. You cannot hold us back!' shouted Gemma, jubilant.

Amir and Dadi watched the children celebrate with huge smiles on their faces. It wasn't over by a long shot but this victory was deserved.

Dadi continued to smile but her thoughts moved to her family at GCI headquarters. Her daughter and two grandsons were there. She hoped they were safe.

•

Kal sat in a chair in the medical wing. Emma and Dr Smythe hovered over him.

'Were you in on it together?' said Emma.

'I don't know what you mean,' answered Kal.

'It was a bold attempt,' admitted Emma. 'I'm almost sorry to see it fail. But so nice of your brother to reveal "The Unlisted" to us, don't you think?'

Kal turned away from her, refusing to make eye contact.

Emma looked at her tablet. 'The *real* discovery is these two chips of yours, Kal. Looking at your test results, I can see you've been performing beyond our expectations for a while now.'

Kal struggled to keep control. 'Isn't that a good thing? Why am I in trouble?'

Emma smiled. 'Oh, you're not in trouble, Kal. Far from it. If I'd known what was possible, I would have double-chipped everyone. I just want to know how you managed to slip under our radar all this time.'

Dr Smythe said, 'Having two chips appears to have given him a superior intellect.'

'Mm, I'm not so sure. If he were that smart he would have turned Dru in to us.' She leaned in closer to Kal. 'Where is he, Kal?'

Kal didn't answer.

Emma looked to the doctor, who adjusted a level on her tablet. 'Increasing control.'

'What are you doing?' asked Kal.

'Don't fight the implants,' she said. 'Give in to them.'

Kal grabbed his head in pain. A moment later his eyes glazed over.

'Full control,' said the doctor, looking at her tablet.

Emma nodded, satisfied.

•

Maya Sharma was also seated in a chair, but she was strapped to it and was in another, less-frequented part of the building.

Emma Ainsworth entered the cell and smiled. 'Dr Sharma,' she said in a creepily friendly voice. 'Always a pleasure.'

'What am I doing here?' Maya demanded.

'I want to thank you for your service. You've been instrumental in the Global Child Initiative's success to date.'

Maya struggled against the straps that trapped her in the chair. 'You have a funny way of saying thanks.'

'I'm particularly interested in the work you've been doing with a certain set of twins,' continued Emma.

That stopped Maya in her tracks.

'In fact, one of your nephews is here to see you now.'

The door opened again, and this time Kal entered. Maya looked to him, hopeful. 'Kal – are you okay?'

Kal was silent.

'Infinity Group appreciates your efforts, Dr Sharma,' said Emma with a fake smile. 'However, we are concerned by the fact you encouraged a troubled teen to leave our facility today.'

Maya feigned ignorance. 'What? I've never done anything like that.'

Emma turned to Kal. 'Kal? Is that true?'

Maya looked at Kal, her eyes pleading.

'My aunt has been helping the Unlisted,' said Kal dispassionately.

Emma nodded.

'Kal!' said Maya, shocked.

'Mm,' said Emma 'That matches a report I received from my people. Rose Aquino's implant was found across the city on a delivery scooter. I wonder how it got there?'

Maya tried to look innocent, but she was well aware her goose was cooked.

Emma turned to Kal. 'Thank you, Kal. Now, tell me the name of your target.'

Kal blinked a couple of times, before answering, 'Drupad Sharma.'

Maya's mouth dropped open in shock. If they could turn identical twins against each other, there was nothing Infinity Group would stop at.

CHAPTER SIXTEEN

Rose and Jacob, with their hoodies pulled up, scurried down an alleyway. As Jacob set to work on one of the walls, Rose peered around a corner towards the main street. She noted a Super Recogniser standing on the street corner, eyeing passers-by.

Looking further to get a view of the whole street, Rose's mouth fell open. There were Super Recognisers on every corner for several blocks.

She retreated back into the alleyway, tapped Jacob on the shoulder and they scuttled away.

A moment later a teenage boy walked past a Super Recogniser and headed down the alley. He stopped short. On the laneway wall was a poster with the words: WE ARE THE UNLISTED. WE ARE COMING. At the bottom of the poster was a QR code. The teen, curious, pulled out a phone and scanned the code. A video appeared on the phone screen, showing four shadowy figures in hoodies. There was a voice over: 'We need you to join us. We need you to stop them.' But before the teen could watch until the end, the video message was suddenly paused. A hand fell on the teen's shoulder. He turned around to find a Super Recogniser standing over him, grim-faced.

•

The sign over Amir's Bollywood cinema advertised old hits including *Raja Hindustani*, *Lagaan* and *Kuch Kuch Hota Hai*. On the cinema's rooftop, an old satellite dish rotated and adjusted with a creak.

Inside the theatre, Dru and Kymara were flipping through pages from the GCI system on Amir's old laptop. Gemma was nearby, picking at a box of popcorn.

'Amazing. We have remote access to the entire GCI mainframe,' said Kymara.

'Broadcasting our message from headquarters was legendary, Dru,' said Gemma.

Dru looked sad. 'It doesn't feel legendary. I left Kal and Bua behind. What's going to happen to them?'

No-one had an answer to that.

Dru saw Kymara flip past a page with information on implants. 'Wait – go back,' he said.

Kymara returned to the previous page. She read out loud, '"Known Technical Flaws. Implants have been shown to lose effectiveness underground, and in close proximity to shortwave emissions of 9351 kilohertz." Next!'

'Hang on. That's interesting,' said Dru, nerding out over the possibilities. 'We already know about the implant not working underground, but shortwave emissions? That could really help us. It's an analogue override!'

Rose and Jacob entered the theatre following their poster drop. When they pulled their hoods down, revealing their faces, Rose looked a bit spooked. 'There are Super Recognisers everywhere. It's getting harder and harder for us to go outside without getting caught.'

'It's the posters. I told you they were a bad idea,' said Gemma.

Jacob disagreed strongly. 'We're done running, Gemms. Now we're showing Infinity Group *they* should be scared of *us*. Right, Rose?'

Rose met Gemma's eyes, and Gemma saw more hope than certainty. 'I –'

'No *way*!' interrupted Kymara with excitement.

Everyone looked to Kymara, who had been tapping away at the laptop throughout.

'Dru. The reason the mainframe didn't stay down for you is you attacked a dummy interface. The real system is hidden underneath.'

'Seriously?' said Dru, looking at Kymara's screen.

Rose was thinking. 'So, does that mean we can shut down the real system before the Global Child Congress tomorrow?'

'Yeah, I think so,' said Kymara, still reading, 'but not remotely. Someone's gonna have to go back to headquarters.'

'Again?' asked Gemma, concerned.

The others groaned.

Dru was also reading onscreen. 'There's a mobile master control device, which Emma Ainsworth is planning on carrying at Government House for the Congress.'

'So, we have to destroy her device and the mainframe at exactly the same time,' said Kymara, frowning. 'If we're off by even a minute, all implanted kids will auto-switch to mind control. Permanently.'

The Unlisted looked at each other, letting these words sink in.

'Wombat?' said Dadi, coming into the theatre, holding her mobile phone out towards Dru. 'A call for you. It's my other wombat. Don't worry – I didn't tell him anything,' she said, handing the phone to Dru. He tentatively put the phone to his ear as the four Unlisted and Dadi watched.

'Kal? Is Bua with you? Did they hurt you?'

On the other end of the phone, Kal replied, 'I'm fine. Where are you? I'll come to you.'

Dru paused for a moment, wary. 'Are they listening?'

'No-one's listening,' answered Kal. 'I'm at home.'

'How did you get away?' asked Dru.

'They let me go. Where are you?'

Dru was incredulous. 'They just let you go? But the guards were chasing me. It seemed like they knew –'

'They don't know anything, Dru. Give me your address. I need to come to you. Now.'

Dru shook his head. 'I'm sorry, Kal. I trust you . . . I just don't trust Emma Ainsworth.' He ended the call and looked to the others, his voice wavering. 'They've got to him. Kal's theirs now.'

•

The Sharma house was unusually quiet as the front door swung open and Rahul and Anousha stepped in. They stood in the hallway, listening for movement. Nothing. 'No-one's home?' said Rahul.

Anousha smiled. 'A morning to ourselves at last! Come here, you gorgeous man.' Anousha was about to kiss her husband when she saw Kal out of the corner of her eye. He was sitting on the couch in the lounge room, dressed in his school uniform.

'Kal,' said Anousha. 'You're home.'

Kal turned towards his parents with a blank expression. 'Have you seen Dru?'

'He's out with Dadi in the food truck, feeding vulnerable kids,' said Anousha.

Rahul added, 'We thought you'd be with them.'

Kal nodded and stood up. 'Thank you.' With that, he walked out of the lounge room, leaving his parents bemused by his cold behaviour.

Rahul called out after him, 'Good to have you home with us!'

Kal went to open the front door.

Rahul went after him. 'Everyone else is out – and we've got the day off. The three of us could do something fun.'

'That's nice, Mum and Dad. But I have to be somewhere,' said Kal.

Anousha watched her son closely, with concern. 'When was the last time we spent the day together?' she asked him.

But Kal simply went to open the front door, just as they all heard a knock. Rahul moved quickly ahead of Kal to open the door – to see Emma Ainsworth on their doorstep. Rahul and Anousha were beyond surprised to see this corporate powerhouse in front of them.

Anousha stuttered, 'Oh . . . you're . . .'

'Emma Ainsworth,' Emma said with a confident smile. She shook hands with Rahul and Anousha firmly, professionally. 'It's a pleasure, Mr and Mrs Sharma. I wondered if you had a few minutes.'

'Of course,' said Rahul, looking at his wife in amazement.

Emma Ainsworth nodded to Kal, and he headed out the door. 'Excuse me.'

'Kal?' said Anousha, not keen to let him out of her sight.

Emma interjected. 'Kalpen has preparations to

complete for tomorrow's Congress. Shall we move inside to chat?'

Kal walked purposefully down the driveway without a backward glance. Anousha looked after him, worried, and then shut the door.

CHAPTER SEVENTEEN

'What are you doing?' asked Rose.

Surprised, Dru looked around to see Rose sitting on the snack bar of the cinema, watching him as he stood psyching himself up to leave. 'I'll be right back,' he answered.

'Right after the Super Recognisers take you in?' said Rose dryly.

'Kal's going to find us, Rose,' said Dru. 'And when he does, we're done. We won't make it to the Global Child Congress tomorrow.'

'So, you're running away?' asked Rose, incredulous.

'No. Of course not. Kymara and I found out there's a radio frequency that disables the implants. One of the labs at school has radio components. And I reckon that's the only way we're going to get through to Kal now.'

Rose sighed. 'I get how hard this must be for you. I mean, he's your identical twin.'

Before she could continue, Jacob stuck his head into the lobby. 'I think you might want to see this,' he said.

All the kids, along with Vidya, Dadi and Amir crowded together in the theatre to watch the news streaming on Amir's laptop. A newsreader was onscreen in front of a graphic that read: WHO ARE THE UNLISTED? 'Across Sydney,' she began, 'municipal councils have been working overtime to remove a crop of mysterious posters with one simple message: "We are the Unlisted. We are coming."' As the newsreader continued speaking, footage of the poster was displayed.

'My poster is famous!' announced Amir, proud of his handiwork.

On the screen, someone used a phone to scan the QR code. The video of the four Unlisted kids in black hoodies appeared on the phone.

The newsreader continued: 'Believed to be the work of a vigilante group, the posters all contain a QR code, which links to a cryptic video outlining a "manifesto" of sorts. Recent reports suggest the group may now be spawning copycats as far afield as Paris, Beijing and Moscow.'

The screen showed amateur footage of kids in black hoodies running through city streets, putting up their own versions of the 'We Are Coming' posters.

Jacob was wide-eyed. 'People are copying us?'

'Authorities are watching events closely as they unfold, working to determine whether the "Unlisted" pose a threat to public safety,' finished the newsreader.

Dadi muted the laptop. 'Word is getting out, little ones!'

Gemma nodded. 'If I were Emma Ainsworth, I'd be scared right now.'

Rose turned to Kymara. 'You've been in touch with the other Unlisted kids online, right?'

'Sure have,' said Kymara. 'They're the ones hosting our "manifesto" video.'

'Do you think they could get a call out for more kids? The copycats?' asked Rose.

'I don't see why not,' she said.

Dru looked at Rose. 'What are you thinking?'

Rose stood up. 'I'm thinking you and I have to get to your school as soon as possible.'

Vidya looked at her little brother and his friend. 'If you're going to go out in broad daylight, I'm going to need to give you both a makeover!' Her eyes sparkled.

Rose and Dru looked at each other. *Huh?*

•

At the Sharma house Dru and Kal's parents sat in their lounge groom, politely sipping tea with Emma Ainsworth.

'You should be very proud of your son. He has exceeded all academic expectations within the Global Child Initiative,' said Emma.

'That's amazing,' said Anousha.

'Dru always has been quite a clever boy,' said Rahul.

'I'm talking about Kal,' said Emma.

'Kal?' said Rahul.

'Kal?' repeated Anousha, this time genuinely surprised. If it were sporting prowess, sure, of course Kal was great, but Emma was talking about academic achievement. Anousha wasn't even sure Kal got around to doing his homework!

Emma continued. 'We would be honoured if you could join Kal at the Global Child Congress tomorrow. We see the Sharmas as our model family.'

Rahul and Anousha exchanged a proud look. 'We'll be there. Of course.'

'And there's one other thing . . .' Emma Ainsworth opened a laptop on the coffee table. A beautifully rendered 3D image of a boarding school appeared onscreen. 'This is Highgate,' said Emma, showing the Sharmas the impressive online prospectus. 'The facility is about to open and we're looking at scholarship students now. It would be perfect for Kal.'

'Scholarship?' asked Anousha.

'It wouldn't cost you a thing,' purred Emma. 'It's a state-of-the-art educational facility. Boarding there will allow Kal to truly fulfil his destiny.'

Rahul frowned. 'It looks amazing, but are you saying there's no way the boys can go together?'

Emma shook her head. 'If only Dru had better all-round scores. We need the best and brightest. But that's not to say there isn't a future for Dru. We have other programs.'

Anousha hesitated. 'We're worried about separating the twins. Although they've always been independent of each other to a certain extent, they've never really been apart.'

Emma raised an eyebrow. 'At this stage it's vital they forge their own paths.' She slid a contract over the table to them like the consummate saleswoman. 'Kal belongs at Highgate, Mr and Mrs Sharma. Please trust the Global Child Initiative with your talented son's wellbeing.'

Anousha hesitated for a moment, but she saw Emma's encouraging smile, and slowly signed the contract. Rahul signed after his wife, not quite sure he was making the right decision but not knowing why.

Emma took the signed contract from them and stood, very pleased with herself and her mighty powers of persuasion.

•

Two people who looked very unlike Rose and Dru snuck down an alleyway, with Vidya close behind. Vidya had used her prosthetic make-up skills to create oversized noses, pointy chins and unusual eyebrows. The teens looked more like characters from *The Hobbit* than urban teenagers.

Vidya looked closely at them. 'Those disguises will help protect you from being identified by drones or surveillance cameras but they won't convince a human. Don't let anyone stop you.'

Rose and Dru nodded, then waited as Vidya went out to the main street and looked out.

Jacob and Gemma were at the next block. Vidya nodded to them and they pulled up their hoods, then ran out to put a poster on a wall in the street.

A Super Recogniser saw them and shouted, then took off at a run in their direction. Gemma and Jacob quickly finished putting up the poster and sprinted up an escalator.

Vidya motioned to Rose and Dru, who were now free to go out onto the main street. 'Good luck,' she said.

Rose and Dru ambled down the footpath, trying to look inconspicuous. Meanwhile, the Super Recogniser sprinted up the escalator after Gemma and Jacob and found four other kids wearing black hoodies. 'Stop right there!' she said.

The kids turned around and stared at the Super Recogniser. They were not the kids she had just seen. She seemed confused for a moment but then turned behind her to see two other kids in black hoodies run the other way. 'You two – stop!' she called out and ran over to them. Again, they were two other random kids.

Jacob and Gemma slipped safely down another escalator undetected, watching as more and more teens wearing black hoodies caused havoc in the area.

CHAPTER **EIGHTEEN**

Dru and Rose, still disguised under rubber and make-up, clambered through the window into the science lab at Westbrook High School, then headed towards the electronics equipment.

'We'll need a little of everything,' said Dru. They began loading the satchel with electrical components.

When they'd got everything they needed, they headed back out into the sunshine. This was the pupil-free day before the Global Child Congress, so there were no students around. But when they rounded a corner they ran into Regan sweeping a corner of the quadrangle in her newly acquired yellow tie. She jumped in fright when she saw them. 'What happened to your face?' she asked in alarm.

'My sister,' said Dru wryly.

Looking around, Rose slipped a poster from her satchel and stuck it up on the wall.

Regan wasn't happy. 'You shouldn't have let me see you. The control's getting stronger. I can't trust myself anymore.'

'Don't worry, Regan. I never trusted you in the first place,' said Dru.

'Very funny, Sharma,' retorted Regan with an almost smile.

Dru held a finger to his lips and he and Rose slipped away.

Regan's eyes turned to the poster Rose had put on the wall. Curious, she took out her phone and scanned the code. A video, showing the four shadowy figures in hoodies, loaded on her phone. 'We need you to join us. We need you to stop them. We are the Unlisted – and together we will take back our world.'

A hand fell on Regan's shoulder. Hiding her phone behind her back, she spun around. 'Uh . . . hi, Kal. What are you doing here?'

'Have you seen Dru?' he asked, staring intensely at his classmate.

'He's not at school. You shouldn't be here either.' But the implant was forcing her to tell the truth and she mumbled, 'I . . . I saw him . . .'

Kal stepped closer to Regan. 'Tell me what you know, or I'll report you to Mr Cunningham.'

The threat was too much for Regan. She pointed to the poster. Kal ripped it from the wall. On the other side of the poster was an advertisement for the Bollywood cinema. Recognition registered in Kal's eyes.

Regan glanced at her phone, which was still playing the video. Rose's voice rang out: 'Stand with us. Together we fight and together we win.'

Drawing together the last of her will, Regan stepped forwards and pushed Kal into an open doorway. She closed the two glass doors, and shoved the broom through the handles, locking him in. She knew it wouldn't hold him for long, but it would give Dru and Rose time to get further away from the school.

Kal was furious, banging on the closed door. 'Open the door! Now!'

Moments later Mr Cunningham and two GCI security guards appeared, attracted by the ruckus. 'What's going on here?' he barked.

'Mr Cunningham. Let me out!' yelled Kal from behind the door. Mr Cunningham gestured to the guards and they removed the broom from the door handles. Kal strode out and handed Mr Cunningham the poster he'd ripped down from the school wall.

Regan's shoulders sagged. She wasn't sure what was going to happen now, but she knew it wasn't going to be good.

•

Dru and Rose made it back to the cinema without further incident, and Dru immediately started to work feverishly on building a small device, following a blueprint on the laptop screen before him. Before long he clicked the final piece into place. 'There,' he said triumphantly as he held up his handiwork.

'Is that it?' said Rose, a little unimpressed, as she inspected what looked like a miniature circuit board with a couple of wires attached to it.

'This should block Kal's implant,' said Dru simply. 'It's enough.'

'If we can get close enough to put it on him,' said Kymara doubtfully.

'I'll handle that,' said Dru. 'If Kal's out of action, there's a chance we'll get through tomorrow.'

Rose looked at the others. 'Everyone got the plan?'

They nodded, but before they could discuss details they all heard a bang from the direction of the foyer.

'What was that?' said Gemma, immediately scared.

'Don't worry, I'll take a look,' said Amir, and he bounded out of the auditorium and downstairs into the foyer. The banging continued as Amir approached the glass front door. 'Take it easy! These hinges won't hold –'

On the other side of the door was Kal, a cold look in his eyes.

'Kal!' said Amir, surprised.

Dru rushed down the stairs into the foyer, followed by Kymara, Gemma, Jacob and Vidya. 'Uncle Amir, no! Don't let him in,' Dru shouted, but it was too late. Amir had opened the door. The Unlisted ran back up the stairs and out of sight.

Kal lurched inside the cinema and pushed Amir out of the way. Amir tried to grab Kal's leg but Kal shook him off and ran upstairs in the direction of the auditorium.

He swung the doors open into the theatre. It was dark except for the Bollywood film flickering onscreen. The auditorium seemed empty. Kal called out into the darkness. 'Dru!'

Slivers of light revealed Dru, the Unlisted, Dadi and Vidya hiding in the shadows.

Dru nudged Rose. He held out his walkie-talkie and whispered to her to take her walkie-talkie up to the projection room.

'Dru! Come out!' ordered Kal.

Rose scurried along the wall towards the projection room.

Kal peered into the darkness.

'What's happened to you, wombat? You're scaring me!' Dadi called out.

For a moment, there was a flicker of doubt in Kal's eyes. He blinked. But could not be swayed for long. 'Where is Dru, Dadi?'

Suddenly, Dru's voice boomed around the auditorium. 'Kal! What are you doing?'

The voice seemed as though it came from behind the screen, and Kal bounded down towards it.

Silhouettes and feet scurried in the shadows.

Kal looked behind the screen. Dru's voice was coming from the large speakers.

He turned, looking up to the light in the projection booth. Adjacent to the small room, Dru and the others were hidden. He spoke into the walkie-talkie. 'Kal! You've let the implant control you! Come back to us. We need your help.'

Dru took his finger off the button and whispered to Kymara, Jacob, Gemma, Rose, Dadi and Vidya. 'We have to lead him away. Is there another way out?'

Dadi pointed in the direction of the screen and whispered. 'The fire exit is that way.'

Dru nodded. 'Unlisted, let's go.'

Dadi looked at Dru. 'Don't let him do anything he'll regret.'

'I won't, Dadiji,' said Dru.

Vidya patted her brother's shoulder. 'See you at the emergency meeting point at three o'clock.'

'Go. We'll find a way to slow him down,' said Dadi.

The Unlisted scurried down the opposite aisle as Kal, realising that he had been fooled, bounded up the stairs to the projection box.

He flung the door open. Inside, a live PA microphone sat on Amir's desk, the walkie-talkie positioned next to it. Kal yelled out in frustration. 'Dru!'

Meanwhile, as Dadi and Vidya hid in the theatre, the Unlisted and Dru silently crept behind the screen. On the other side, amid a bunch of old rubbish, Dru opened the fire door to reveal an alleyway.

They spilled out onto the street, eyes blinking as they adjusted to the sunlight.

They started running but Dru stopped and looked behind him. Rose doubled back, and grabbed him.

'I just can't believe we're running from Kal,' Dru said, emotional.

'Right now that's not Kal. Come on. Hurry.' They ran around the corner and after the others.

CHAPTER NINETEEN

Dadi and Vidya remained hidden in the shadows of the auditorium seats, eyes wide, breath shallow.

Kal left the projection room and stormed down the aisle to search the cinema. As he passed his sister's hiding spot, Vidya stuck her arm out, grabbing Kal's ankle. He tripped, and scrambled to regain his balance.

Dadi used the opportunity to stand over him. 'You naughty little thing. Bursting in here to make a mess. Fighting with your twin brother like a spoiled toddler! Your parents will ground you until you are middle-aged.'

Kal looked around, confused. 'Where did they go?'

Vidya's eyes flicked to the screen involuntarily. Following her gaze, Kal leapt to his feet, running up to the screen and out the door.

Dadi's heartbreak was clear. 'My poor little wombats! I hope Dru knows what he's doing.'

•

Kal didn't take long to catch up to Dru and the Unlisted. He knew they would be avoiding main roads, and the alleyway system was easy to follow.

Kymara, up ahead, looked back and saw him approaching. 'He's coming!'

The five kids quickened their pace. Gemma tripped over a stack of milk crates and fell. Jacob ran back to help her to her feet. She got up and started running but Kal was sprinting right at Jacob. Jacob stood firm to block Kal's way. 'Kal, stop! It's us!'

But Kal was too strong. 'Get out of my way, Jacob,' he said as he pushed Jacob to one side and kept sprinting towards the others, his eyes fixed on his twin.

'He's only after me!' said Dru. 'If I stay with you we'll all be in danger.' He bolted off on his own, leaving the others behind.

'Wait! Dru!' shouted Kymara.

'Dru!' echoed Gemma, but he was already sprinting down an alleyway and disappearing into the heart of the city.

As Kal got closer, Rose, Gemma and Kymara tipped rubbish bins in his path, trying to slow him down.

He jumped one and stumbled on the next, slowing briefly. But arms pumping, eyes fixed, he kept running, ignoring the girls, focused only on chasing his brother.

Dru was panting hard, almost out of breath, sprinting hard through city laneways. He skidded around a corner and ducked into a doorway just in time to hide from Kal, who sprinted down the laneway, barrelling past Dru's hiding place.

Dru quickly doubled back, emerging in the busy street at the other end, concealing himself briefly in the bustling, passing pedestrian traffic.

Kal stopped, realising he had lost the trail. He turned around, unable to see Dru. But he noticed the entrance to the tunnels. A thought came to him and he backtracked, returning to the laneway at a sprint. He ran up a staircase, full of energy. He got to the top of the overpass that led towards the tunnel entrance. Here, he had a great view of the city below him. Up ahead, he saw Dru in the distance, jogging away from him.

Kal smiled.

•

Rose cautiously peered out of a Chinatown alleyway. She spotted the Indian food truck driven by Dadi. Signalling back to Gemma, Kymara and Jacob who had remained hidden, Rose stepped out towards the truck but was stopped by Gemma, who nodded towards two Super Recognisers on the other side of the road.

The food truck pulled up and the back doors opened. Vidya jumped out. She looked around, but it wasn't until she heard a whistle that she looked into the alleyway and saw the Unlisted waiting in an alcove. She nodded for Rose and the others to get in, then she turned and walked over to a couple of Super Recognisers.

'Hey! Recognise me?' asked Vidya, being loud and obnoxious.

The Super Recogniser coughed and gestured for her to move aside.

Vidya wasn't going anywhere. 'Come on, come on, you can't hide. I see you and all your creepy friends!' she yelled. 'Am I on your list too? *We see you!*'

As she made a commotion, the Unlisted, one by one, sprinted across the street unnoticed. Rose, Kymara, then Gemma.

The Super Recogniser glared at Vidya. 'Get lost, kid.'

Vidya ended her rant with, 'We've got our eyes on you,' and ran back towards the van, quite proud of her performance. Now out of sight of the Super Recognisers, she jumped in the van, slammed the doors shut and banged on the wall of the vehicle. Dadi hit the accelerator and the truck sped off.

'That was close,' said Gemma.

Kymara looked at everyone else, dread written on her face. 'Where's Jacob?'

They looked out the back window of the van to see Jacob being detained by one of the Super Recognisers.

Rose, Kymara and Gemma's faces registered utter shock as they realised they'd accidentally left him behind.

•

Kal arrived at the tunnel entrance. The gate had been pulled open but Dru was nowhere to be seen. Kal peered into the darkness of the tunnels.

'Dru!'

There was no answer. He waited a moment longer, and then entered.

'Dru! Come out!' he yelled, his voice echoing down the tunnel.

Kal waited for his eyes to adjust to the darkness.

'Dru . . . I know you're in here.' He walked on.

Eventually, echoing from deep in the tunnel, came Dru's voice. 'Kal?'

Kal stopped, listening.

Dru continued. 'Kal. I know you're still in there somewhere. Whatever part of you is listening, please . . .'

Kal walked deeper into the tunnel. His fingers twitched as his implant was affected, but his pace didn't slow.

'The implant is weaker down here. And you're stronger than they are. You're better than they are.'

Up ahead in the darkness, Dru hid in the shadows. He held the blocking device in his hand. 'Kal?' Because of his nerves, Dru fumbled as he raised the device in the direction of Kal's footfalls and it fell to the ground. Dru gasped. *No!* He reached down to pick it up but saw it had landed in a puddle. The water would kill the circuitry. It would be as good as useless until it dried out. Dru tried to stem his rising panic as he sensed Kal moving closer. He cleared his throat and continued talking.

'You'd never hurt me, Kal. We're connected. You know that, right?'

A glimmer of light flicked in Kal's eyes. His footsteps slowed.

'You saved my life. Remember?'

Kal stopped.

Dru knew he had to keep talking. 'When we were ten. You woke up in the middle of the night calling my name. I wasn't in my bed, and everyone started running around like crazy looking for me. But you went straight outside. I was sleepwalking . . . about to step onto the road. Mum said when they woke me up I just said, "Thanks Kal."'

Dru stepped out from the shadows and faced his brother, square on. 'We're connected. We're more than brothers . . . we're twins.'

Kal's eyes glistened in the dark. Dru couldn't tell whether he was experiencing emotion, or it was an implant glitch. He started moving again, and Dru looked nervously at his brother's approaching silhouette.

'I can't do it without you, bro,' said Dru. 'I can't take on Ainsworth without your help. I need you.'

Kal ran straight towards his brother.

CHAPTER **TWENTY**

The day of the Global Child Congress had arrived. At Government House, brightly coloured banners boasting photos of healthy young people and slogans such as THE FUTURE IS NOW and A WHOLE CHILD MEANS A BETTER FUTURE FOR ALL adorned the front of the building.

Kal led Dru roughly through the building, flanked by Infinity Group security guards. Kal pushed Dru into the grand entrance hall, where Dru slumped groggily to the floor.

'Wonderful, he's here,' said Emma Ainsworth as she entered the hall, dressed in a bright orange power suit.

'He fell and hit his head,' said Kal to Emma. 'Still a bit shaky.'

'Thank you, Kal. No harm done, I'm sure,' said Emma sweetly.

Dru looked up, bleary and weak. 'This won't work.'

Emma disagreed. 'It already has, Dru – you're here. You're an impressive boy. It would be a pity to waste a brain like yours.' She nodded to a guard. 'Take him away.' And then she turned to Kal. 'And let's get you cleaned up.' She and Kal walked away as the guard grabbed a weak Dru and dragged him through the doorway into a secure room.

•

With a squeal of tyres and loud Bollywood music blaring, the Indian food truck raced into the GCI car park, stopping directly at the front of the impressive building.

Kymara was wedged into a tiny space behind the front seats, Amir's old laptop at the ready. 'I can zonk their security system long enough to get you in,' she said to Gemma, 'but you'll have to move fast.'

Gemma nodded.

Dadi opened the driver's door. 'My samosas and I are on the case.'

Vidya and Dadi opened the food truck for business, putting a dish of warm samosas out on the service counter. Smelling the food, a couple of GCI guards came over, including one who was very familiar with Dadi's cooking.

'Hello again,' said the guard to Dadi.

'Dear me, you're looking thin. Are they feeding you at home?'

'You can't really park here,' the guard said, although his resolve trailed off as the aroma seduced him. 'Is that roasted cumin?'

'Impressive! You must have a samosa,' said Dadi. 'On the house.'

Vidya smiled. 'Coming right up.' She handed a samosa to Dadi who covered it with fresh onion and chutney.

'All the toppings for my favourite Global Child Initiative guard,' said Dadi as she passed it to him.

'Mm,' he said after the first bite, 'the tamarind in the chutney!'

Another officer stepped up and Dadi handed him a samosa too. The guard got on his radio. 'Attention all stations . . . there's some killer food here in the car park.'

Dadi and Vidya smiled happily. 'I hope we have enough for all of you!'

The guard shrugged. 'Not many of us here today – most are at some fancy launch at Government House.'

A few officers arrived outside the food truck and soon all were chugging down samosas.

While they were distracted, Gemma crept out of the van. She looked back at Kymara, who gave her a thumbs up, then Rose pulled the van door closed.

Gemma ran ahead into the building without being noticed.

Halfway through his second samosa, Dadi's favourite guard's stomach gurgled loudly. He grabbed his belly, looking concerned. 'Um . . . excuse me one second,' he said and made a quick waddle towards the building.

It didn't take long for the other security guards to feel similarly off-colour. After a couple of serious stomach cramps, they all headed inside to the bathrooms in the main foyer.

Dadi and Vidya gave each other a high-five. Stage one complete.

Inside the building, Gemma made her way down a corridor. 'I'm in,' she reported via the walkie-talkie.

Inside the food truck Kymara was looking at the map of headquarters on the laptop. Rose sat next to her. Over the walkie-talkie, Kymara offered directions. 'Take a right, then the second left. And down the stairs. Then it'll be the first door you see.'

Gemma ran down the stairs and rounded the corner. There was a room there but the door wouldn't budge. She pushed on it. Nothing. 'Door's locked,' she said.

'Hold on, I'm trying something,' said Kymara through the walkie-talkie. Then less than a minute later she added: 'Try it now.'

Gemma tried again – and the door opened on a featureless room. 'Jacob?'

There was definitely someone in the room, but it turned out to be Dr Sharma. She looked strained and tired.

'Gemma! Is Dru with you?' asked Maya.

'No. We haven't heard from him since yesterday. We think Kal caught him.'

The walkie-talkie crackled. 'Gemms?' said Rose. 'You got Jacob?'

'No, but I found the twins' aunt. Jacob must be in another room.'

Kymara came over the air: 'I'm opening all the doors. You've got fifteen seconds to find him before the security override locks me out.'

Gemma and Maya raced along the corridor, opening doors. All the rooms were empty.

They could hear Kymara's voice over the walkie-talkie counting down: 'Five . . . four . . . three . . . two . . .'

In the final second, Gemma threw open the last door in the corridor to reveal Jacob wearing a white jumpsuit, sitting on a single bed.

Jacob looked up with a grin. 'You took your time.'

CHAPTER TWENTY-ONE

Emma and Kal, flanked by two Global Child Initiative security guards, walked out onto the front steps of Government House. Emma held a shiny black leather case close to her. Kal had now changed into a smart grey uniform with a matching tie and linen blazer with orange ribbons on the lapels.

Below them, on the lawn of Government House, members of the press mixed with VIPs, business people, Infinity Group investors and international dignitaries. Photographers snapped pictures that would appear tomorrow in newspapers and online all over the world.

'This is it, Kal,' said Emma, looking at the crowd. 'Everything we've been working towards.'

'Yes, Ms Ainsworth.'

'You won't remember this conversation after today, but I want you to know – I think you're the Initiative's greatest achievement.'

'Yes, Ms Ainsworth.'

Kal's eyes quickly glanced to the case in Emma's hand and then back at the guests on the lawn.

Emma spotted Rahul and Anousha Sharma, who were dressed up and looking very excited to be at such an auspicious event. 'Mr and Mrs Sharma,' Emma said as she led Kal to them. 'So great to see you again. Having a good time?'

'Absolutely,' replied Anousha.

Rahul agreed. 'I've always wanted to be invited to Government House. I thought I'd have to wait until I became Governor.'

'Well, you'd have our support,' said Emma with a laugh. 'And where's the rest of your wonderful family?'

'They had a sleepover with their grandmother,' answered Rahul.

'They'll be joining us soon,' added Anousha. 'I hope.'

'I'm particularly keen to see Dru. Aren't you, Kal?' asked Emma Ainsworth, the picture of innocence.

Kal nodded, avoiding eye contact with his parents. 'Dru's important to all of us.'

Anousha tried to catch her son's eye.

'Please excuse us. We should speak with the guests,' said Emma, ushering Kal away from his confused parents.

•

When Emma and Kal had moved out of earshot, Anousha turned to her husband and said quietly, 'Why do you think Dru's pretending to be Kal?'

Rahul shrugged. 'Beats me.'

'Should we be worried?' asked Anousha.

But Rahul didn't get a chance to answer as the crowds were ushered towards the lectern, where the New South Wales Governor was waiting to begin formal proceedings.

•

The Indian food truck had closed for business outside GCI headquarters, and Dadi was now driving Rose, Kymara and Vidya across town.

Kymara was no longer crouched down between the seats, but she still had Amir's laptop open and ready. 'Gemms,' she said into the walkie-talkie. 'You got my instructions?'

At headquarters, Gemma, flanked by Jacob and Bua, came down a corridor on the first floor. Gemma pulled a piece of paper from her pocket and unfolded it. It was covered in handwritten notes from Kymara.

'Yep,' Gemma replied. 'Now we have to work out how to get into the mainframe room.'

Rose checked her watch and spoke into the walkie-talkie. 'You should still have some time before the guards are back in action.'

Gemma, Jacob and Bua stopped and looked below them, into the main foyer. A couple of guards were walking from the bathroom back to their station when they both clutched their stomachs, groaning, and jogged back to the bathroom.

Gemma laughed. 'Yeah – I reckon we've still got some time. We've just seen some guards coming out of the bathroom and, man, they don't look happy. What did Dadi put in those samosas anyway?'

Rose giggled. 'You don't want to know. Anyway, we're about to arrive at Government House. We'll call through when we've smashed Emma Ainsworth's master control.'

'Sure,' said Gemma. 'But just hold on a sec.'

They heard a rustle, then the walkie-talkie came to life: 'Hi guys,' came Jacob's voice. 'Have you missed me?'

Of course they had, but they weren't about to tell him that.

'Not so much,' said Kymara with a big grin. 'We've just been cruising around, you know.'

Her comment coincided with a sharp turn Dadi had taken with the Kombi, and Kymara and Rose went flying in the back of the van. 'Whhoooooa!' said Rose.

'I'm sorry, emus,' said Dadi. 'It was an amber light and I didn't want to get a ticket for going through a red.'

Vidya looked at her Dadi driving. 'I'm telling Mum and Dad I want you to teach me how to drive from now on, Dadi. We'll have much more fun.'

Dadi frowned, beeping her horn at a pedestrian who'd decided to walk out in front of the van. 'We'll see,' she said.

Back at headquarters, Jacob decided to offer some timely advice over the walkie-talkie. 'Remember,' said Jacob through the walkie-talkie, 'you need to try to smash the master control before she zombifies all those kids, okay?'

'Yeah. Thanks, Jacob,' replied Rose sarcastically. But it was good to hear his voice again and know that he was safe.

•

The Governor of New South Wales, the Honourable Salma Hernandez, stood at a lectern and microphone, beneath a tasteful GCI banner.

Assembled before her, press, investors and dignitaries listened intently.

'Welcome, distinguished visitors, members of the press, teachers. And to parents – the people who give us the gift of a bright future through their precious children.'

There was a round of warm applause.

Dru stood off to the side with Emma. She did not see his eyes move to his parents, or the way they watched him, puzzlement clear on their faces. She had only one focus today, and so far everything was going to plan.

Salma continued. 'It is with great pleasure as your Governor that I introduce a woman who has worked tirelessly to make the Global Child Initiative a reality – Emma Ainsworth!'

Huge cheers and applause.

Emma stepped up to the microphone. 'Thank you. Thank you. You're very kind, Governor. What a privilege it is to stand here today. I feel humbled to be part of this program, to be present with such inspiring young people. Everything. Changes. Today.'

Another round of applause.

'Please join me in welcoming the pupils of Westbrook High School, model students in the Global Child Initiative,' continued Emma.

A stirring drum roll sounded as the students marched together in school uniforms and in formation. They arranged themselves quickly and efficiently in Basic and Core groups. The audience members did not know what Emma knew, so they were unlikely to register the matching glazed-eye look the students all wore.

Tim and Chloe, the Elites, stood to attention in front of the class.

All the students opened their mouths and spoke with one voice. 'Welcome to the future.'

The audience applauded.

'We have seen unprecedented improvement in all academic and athletic fields,' said Emma, 'at Westbrook and across the nation. And things are only going to get better. Today I am excited to announce . . . for our most gifted students . . .' Dramatic music built up as 3D graphics of a huge, ultra-modern, residential complex appeared behind Emma. 'Highgate Academy. The residential education facility of tomorrow.'

The audience were collectively impressed, with gasps and sounds of delight.

'One of Highgate's very first students is right here on this stage with me. To tell you about his experiences with the Global Child Initiative, I present the truly extraordinary Kalpen Sharma.'

There was solid applause.

Emma gestured for the boy to step up to the lectern. She spoke into his ear. 'Don't worry, Kal. You'll find the words within you.'

He nodded, then looked at the expectant faces in the audience and moved over to the microphone. Emma watched him carefully, mildly concerned at the sweat and discomfort she discerned. He started speaking and then cleared his throat loudly into the microphone. 'The Global Child Initiative is . . .'

He trailed off and put one hand to his head. 'Uh . . . I'm sorry.' His words echoed over the sound system.

Emma watched, growing ever more concerned. Was there something wrong with the implant? The speech should have been delivered straight to the boy's brain.

The boy continued. 'The Global Child Initiative is . . . good. And Highgate is also good. Everything is very, very . . . good.'

Emma was trying hard not to grimace. This was obviously another glitch in the system. Today was *not* the day for glitches, not with all their high-net-worth investors out in the crowd.

The boy on stage wiped the sweat from his brow. The audience, including the boy's parents, looked confused. Something was clearly wrong.

Emma decided to draw things to a close quickly and started clapping. 'Thank you, Kalpen, thank you.'

The crowd started clapping half-heartedly after her as the boy stepped back from the lectern, looking more than a little terrified.

CHAPTER TWENTY-TWO

With the curtains to the food truck closed, Rose was preparing Dadi for the next step in their plan. Gone were the tainted samosas. Dadi was now dressed in a beautiful ruby silk sari, with a garland of marigolds around her neck. She looked like a princess.

Vidya, holding the walkie-talkie, sat next to Kymara in the back of the van as Kymara tapped away on the laptop. 'How will I know when you've destroyed the master control?' Vidya asked nervously.

'Glad you asked,' said Kymara. 'Got your phone?'

Vidya handed Kymara her phone. As Kymara pointed to the laptop, showing something to Vidya, Rose placed another garland of marigolds around Dadi's neck. It was the finishing touch. 'You look perfect, Dadi. Are you ready?'

'To free my two precious wombats from these dreadful people? I've got this. Is that how you young people say it?'

Rose smiled. 'You've got this, Dadi.'

Dadi squeezed Rose's hand and opened the driver's door. Rose watched her walk regally away from the van and up a path to the main entrance, then she and Kymara hurried out of the van to their designated hiding spot, leaving Vidya alone.

Time for the next part of the plan.

•

'Oh, I *am* sorry I'm so late!' gushed Dadi as she rushed up the steps to the two security guards checking credentials. She went to pass them but the guards stopped her. 'Your pass, please?'

Dadi feigned annoyance. 'Oh, it was in my briefcase. Which I left behind in the taxi.'

The security guards did not look sympathetic. 'We can't let you in without a pass,' said one of them gruffly.

Dadi puffed out her chest. 'I am the head of the Marigold Foundation. We fund the Global Child Initiative to the tune of a hundred million dollars a year. You *must* let me in,' she said officiously.

The guard didn't back down. He remained blocking Dadi's way. Dadi glared at him. 'This is your last day with the Initiative, I can tell you that!' She raised her voice, determined to make a scene. 'Take your hands off me!' she yelled, even though no-one had touched her.

A few people close by turned and stared.

At a nearby side entrance, a security guard was stationed alone but when he saw the commotion at the main gate, he left his post and jogged over to the scene.

As soon as the guard moved, Kymara and Rose snuck out from their hiding place in the bushes. They went through the unguarded side entrance and into the building.

'Ma'am, please. Step back!' the guard said to the hysterical Indian woman.

'This is outrageous!' howled Dadi, refusing to calm down.

•

Back at GCI headquarters, Jacob snuck into the men's toilets. It really didn't smell good but he had something vitally important to do and he was the one to do it. Most of the stalls were occupied and noisy. He thought of Dadi's samosas with a smirk and tried not to think about what was going on behind those cubicle doors.

A toilet flushed, and a man in uniform opened the door and came out. Jacob flattened himself against the wall next to the sinks. There was no time to escape.

Luckily, another sudden cramp disabled the guard and he turned around and raced back into the stall he'd just come out of, locking the door behind him.

Jacob breathed a sigh of relief and lowered himself to the floor. He crawled past the cubicles, looking at the feet underneath the doors. When he reached the third pair of feet, he found what he was looking for: a black security pass hanging from a pair of trousers that were bunched around a pair of white, hairy legs. Carefully reaching under the cubicle, Jacob quickly grabbed the pass, clambered to his feet and ran out of the bathroom, very pleased to be breathing better quality air once more!

•

Now that the official part of the day had finished, the press and public were starting to leave Government House. Emma was chatting with Rahul, while Anousha had a quiet talk with her son.

'What's going on, Dru? What happened on stage?' she asked.

'I get nervous in front of people,' said Dru.

Anousha fixed Dru with a deadly serious look. 'Why are you pretending to be Kal? Is it some sort of prank? I think I should tell Ms Ainsworth.'

'No, Mum. No,' said Dru. 'It's not a prank. I'll explain everything later. Please. You have to trust me on this.' Dru looked at his mother, pleading.

At that moment, Emma Ainsworth interrupted them. 'We have a few plans for Kal this afternoon, but then he'll be home to pack for Highgate. Mr and Mrs Sharma, thank you so much for coming today.'

Smiling, Emma shook hands with Anousha and Rahul in her usual businesslike manner, then led Dru towards Government House. Anousha looked after them, still unsure about whether she should have told Emma Ainsworth about the twin swap. But it was too late now, she decided.

•

The moment Emma entered the formal study the smile dropped from her face, and she turned to stare intently at the teenager in front of her. 'How are you feeling, Kal?'

'Good,' he answered. 'I mean . . . all functions are normal.'

'Your speech to the press was less than optimal. I'll get a technician in here to check your operating status.'

'There's no need,' said Dru quickly.

Emma looked at him, an eyebrow raised, so he continued quickly. 'You've personally made sure everything's in place for the final stage.'

Stroking Emma's ego worked, bringing a look of satisfaction to her face. 'Yes. I have, haven't I?' She held up the master control. 'Take this to the function room for the investors' presentation. It's almost time. I'll join you once I've reported to my superiors.'

'Yes, Ms Ainsworth,' said Dru as she handed him the master control. He turned and left the room, as Emma took out her phone and dialled a number.

Dru walked with the laptop and master control in his hand. He passed two Infinity security guards and nodded to them neutrally. The guards moved around a corner and out of sight. Dru knew his moment had come and there was no time to lose, so he hurried to a nearby side table with a heavy stone ornament sitting on it.

He placed the master control on the floor and lifted the ornament. He was about to bring it down when . . . Rose and Kymara swooped in and tackled him to the floor. 'Now!'

'Wha—' said Dru, madly trying to figure out what just happened.

'Get the control!' yelled Rose as she kept Dru pinned to the floor.

Kymara picked it up and then asked, 'How do I destroy it?'

'Wait,' said Dru, completely frustrated. '*I* was about to destroy it!'

'Hit it with something heavy,' suggested Rose, ignoring her captive. 'Hurry! I took Kal by surprise, but he's not gonna stay down!'

Dru groaned. 'But I'm Dru!'

'Yeah, sure you are,' said Rose.

'Stop talking and let me smash this thing!' said Kymara.

Emma Ainsworth entered the room. 'I'd really prefer you didn't,' she said, her voice ice cold.

All three teens looked up to see Emma flanked by two guards. One of the guards stepped forwards and took the laptop and master control from Kymara.

'Bring me the other one,' said Emma. The guard nodded and left to retrieve Kal from the secure room.

•

Back at headquarters Gemma, Jacob and Maya approached the door to the data control centre, the mainframe of the whole organisation. Gemma used the black pass that Jacob had retrieved and the door clicked open. The trio entered the room to see huge banks of computers, wires and screens. They were overwhelmed by what they saw.

Maya whistled. 'This is way above my pay grade.'

CHAPTER TWENTY-THREE

Emma was quietly furious as she stood over Dru, Kymara and Rose, flanked by one of her guards. The other had been dispatched to fetch 'the other one', but she was not in the mood to share secrets with this trio of teens. She wanted to see their reactions for herself.

'Breaking into a restricted event and attempting to destroy private property. What do you have to say for yourselves? Rose?'

'We have nothing to say to you,' said Rose defiantly from her chair.

'We'll see about that,' said Emma.

The door opened and the other guard returned, dragging in a groggy-looking Kal, as ordered. He was still dressed in Dru's clothes and glasses.

Emma stood back and examined Kal for a moment. She stepped forwards, spotting the loose wire poking out from under one T-shirt sleeve. She lifted the sleeve to reveal the blocking device, taped to Kal's upper arm. Peeling the tape off, she removed the device and dropped it to the floor, crushing it under her heel.

Kal instantly reacted as though he'd been electrocuted. His eyes flickered as the implants started receiving information once more. He took off Dru's glasses and threw them back to his twin, carelessly.

He stood to attention for Emma. 'Ms Ainsworth.'

'Good to see you again, Kal,' said Emma.

Emma turned to the three seated teenagers.

'Clever. Very clever,' she sneered. 'But the game's over now.' Emma spoke to the guards. 'Keep the trespassers in here. I'll deal with them after the presentation.'

Emma gestured at Dru. 'Give that blazer to Kal.'

But before Dru could move, the guard roughly took the blazer off him and handed it to Kal.

Emma gestured to the master control as Kal put the blazer on. 'As planned, Kal, you will activate the master control.'

'It will be my honour.'

'No!' said Rose.

'Kal!' said Kymara.

'If you press that button you'll be gone for good,' warned Dru. 'You can never come back!'

Kal's eyes moved over Dru and the others as if they weren't even there.

Emma opened the door and led Kal away.

•

A core group of dignitaries and investors – the true heart of Infinity Group – were gathered in a large function room. They sat in a semicircle, waiting impatiently for the sign that their significant investment was about to bear fruit.

Tim and Chloe, as Elites, stood off to one side.

Emma entered, followed by Kal, who was wearing the Highgate blazer and standing tall. The dignitaries and investors fell silent in anticipation.

Emma remained standing and addressed the group. 'My fellow visionaries. A few years ago Infinity Group posed a question: In a world of dwindling resources and a changing climate, how do we ensure a peaceful future?' She paused, looking at each investor separately, milking the moment. 'The answer, of course, lies with our children.'

Kal stepped forwards to stand beside Emma as she continued. 'Between the ages of twelve and fourteen, children enter what's known as a "second infancy" – a period of exceptional neuroplasticity. Shape a child's mind at this age, and you have them for life. A generation of powerful workers, enforcers, guardians. And our guarantee for global security and control.'

The dignitaries and investors applauded enthusiastically.

•

Dru, Kymara and Rose were being watched over by two guards.

Dru glared at them. 'You must know what you're doing is wrong,' he said.

They did not reply, but even if they had they would not have been heard over the sudden sound of an Indian woman shouting from outside the building. Everyone looked towards the window.

'Dadi!' Dru whispered to the others triumphantly.

Dadi's voice carried over the fracas. 'This is a complete and utter *disgrace*.'

The guards moved to the window and looked out. 'It is scandalous!' Dadi shouted. 'It is shameful! And it *will not stand!*'

The guard who had dealt with Dadi last time approached her on the lawn. 'Ma'am, I have already asked you once to leave the premises . . .'

'You have dishonoured me today, sir.' said Dadi. 'It's an affront of international proportions!'

The two guards chuckled as they saw their colleagues battle the furious woman wearing a sari. One turned back a second later to check on their prisoners – but the three chairs were now empty and the door was open. The children had escaped.

•

Emma was coming to the end of her speech. 'I promised to deliver total loyalty. Today you have it. Kalpen, tell me how you feel about your twin brother.'

'My brother means nothing to me. Only the Initiative matters,' said Kal.

Appreciative murmurs came from the audience.

'The time has arrived to make this transformation permanent.' Emma held out the master control to Kal. 'Kal, please do the honours.'

But before Kal could take the master control, Dru, Rose and Kymara burst into the room.

'Smash it, Kal – now!' yelled Rose.

'Destroy that box!' shouted Kymara.

'Please, Kal,' said Dru. 'I got through to you in the tunnels. I know you're still in there.'

Kal hesitated, and Emma looked at him, her confident veneer starting to crack. 'Perhaps, under these slightly unusual circumstances, I'll press the button myself.'

The dignitaries and investors shifted in their seats. This wasn't looking good. Someone in the audience said, 'She can't control the child.'

Kal turned and spoke to Dru. 'You didn't get through to me. You used the tunnels, and your blocker, to make me weak.'

'I disabled the implants to reach the real you,' replied Dru.

'The implants *are* the real me. They're the best part of me. I'm smarter now. I'm stronger. And I finally see I don't need you. Or anyone,' said Kal.

Tim and Chloe remained oblivious to the drama around them. They stayed still and expressionless.

Kal turned to Emma, who was watching the conversation play out with fascination. 'Ms Ainsworth. This time it's a fair fight. You can prove once and for all you built something that's more powerful than friends or family.' He held out his hand. 'I'd like to press the button.'

Emma considered his offer. Then she nodded and smiled, and handed him the master control. 'Please. Go right ahead.'

'Kal . . .' warned Rose.

'Don't do this,' said Kymara.

Kal held out a finger to press the button.

Dru gave it one last shot. 'Kal. It's me. I've been here your whole life – and I'm here now. Emma Ainsworth can make you stronger, but she'll always be your master. I just want to be your brother.'

Holding the device in one hand, Kal looked at Dru and paused. Then he looked back to Emma. He reached out for the master switch – and snapped it in two.

There were gasps of horror from the investors.

CHAPTER TWENTY-FOUR

Gemma sat at the mainframe computer at GCI headquarters, typing code as quickly as she could follow Kymara's written instructions. The door to the data control centre – the mainframe of the whole organisation – had opened easily with the black pass that Jacob had liberated from the guard, and now Gemma, along with Maya and Jacob, were waiting for the signal to move to the final stage of the plan. Tension filled the silence as Gemma typed, making sure she copied exactly what Kymara had written down.

Finally, after what seemed like hours, Vidya's voice came over the walkie-talkie. 'They've done it! Repeat: they've done it! Wipe the mainframe!'

'Go for it, Gemma,' Jacob encouraged. 'Before they auto-switch to zombie mode.'

Gemma was still typing furiously. 'Almost there,' she said.

At that moment the door to the data control centre swung inwards and two Infinity security guards tried to enter – but Maya and Jacob used all their weight to keep the door closed.

'Gemma, go! We can't hold them much longer,' said Maya.

Gemma typed the last of the text from the instructions and hit the ENTER key, sending a line of complicated code into the heart of the system. A dialogue box came up onscreen: MAINFRAME COMPROMISED.

She looked at Maya and Jacob. 'I think we did it,' she said, just as the security guards burst in. All the screens were shutting down, one by one. The guards stopped dead in their tracks, not sure what needed to be done now.

•

At Government House, Kal collapsed as the signal to the implants shut down. Dru rushed over to help him, just as Chloe and Tim also collapsed. Rose and Kymara ran to them.

Kymara had Vidya's mobile phone and she nudged Rose. Kymara pressed record and focused on Rose, who stood up tall. 'We have people in your headquarters,' Rose said to a shocked Emma Ainsworth. 'They just wiped your system. Your control is gone.'

Emma pulled herself together. She chuckled. 'Wiped? You think we don't have backups? Our system will be up and running again by this time tomorrow. We have thousands of implanted children across the country. Every one of them will be under our control, and there's nothing – *nothing* – you can do to stop it.'

'You get all that, Kymaniacs?' asked Kymara, holding up the phone to take in the surroundings before focusing back on Emma.

Rose said to Emma, 'Wave to your audience. We're live streaming.'

Dru added, 'Kymara has a lot of followers, and your excellent speech has just been broadcast to thousands of people all over the world. You just confessed to illegally implanting thousands of children with the aim of keeping them under your control.'

Emma hesitated a moment, then turned and ran out the door.

Rose made a move to follow Emma.

'Let her go,' said Dru. 'She's finished.'

Chloe and Tim were starting to feel better. They were groggy but a lot more aware of what was going on around them. Kal, his brother not leaving his side, was still pretty weak, but his large grin made it clear he was fully aware of what he'd been a part of.

The kids could hear sirens approaching, and it didn't take long for the police to arrive outside Government

House. Some of the investors had already snuck out the back entrance to avoid exposure, but before long Infinity Group guards were being marched out of the building.

Dru, Kal, Rose and Kymara made their way to the Kombi van, where they were embraced by a very enthusiastic Dadi. 'My brilliant little wombats!' she cried as she wrapped her arms around the twins.

Maya, Jacob and Gemma, who had been able to leave GCI headquarters with no resistance, soon arrived and ran over to the others. They all hugged, so happy to be reunited.

'We did it! We actually did it!' said Gemma.

'You were amazing. All of you,' said Rose.

Dru patted Kal on the shoulder. 'Especially this fella. Strongest guy I know.'

The kids smiled. Their ordeal was finally over.

CHAPTER TWENTY-FIVE

A few restful days later, the Sharma family sat at the dinner table eating another one of Dadi's feasts. Maya was there too, enjoying quality family time now that she was temporarily unemployed.

The TV was on, and an image of Emma Ainsworth in handcuffs appeared on the screen. 'Oh, turn it up!' said Dru.

A reporter stood outside GCI headquarters. 'Emma Ainsworth, former CEO of Infinity Group, was in court today, facing a number of criminal charges related to the "Implantgate" scandal.' The reporter jostled with other media as a suited man appeared onscreen.

The reporter asked, 'New Chair of the Board, Haru Tanaka . . . you've been swift to distance Infinity Group from any wrongdoing.'

The reporter held the microphone out to Haru Tanaka for his response. 'That's right. After dozens of arrests, an internal review and a clean sweep of the house, I'm proud to say that the culture that allowed this in our organisation is well and truly over.'

Rahul turned off the TV with a sigh.

Vidya wasn't happy. 'So, Infinity Group just keeps going,' she said.

'Yeah, but Emma Ainsworth will be in prison – and she was the evil genius behind it all,' said Maya.

Dru grinned. 'If she's a genius and we beat her, what does that make us?'

Dadi knew the answer, of course. 'Super geniuses!'

'Well, me, at least,' said Kal.

'Hey, hey,' said Rahul. 'Everyone's a super genius in this family. You all follow my example,' he said humbly, then playfully batted away the linen serviettes thrown at him.

Later that evening the twins were using Dru's laptop, having a group video chat with their new friends.

The first window showed Gemma and Rose together. In the second window were Kymara and Jacob. And the third window revealed Jiao, with whom they had reconnected after 'Implantgate' was revealed.

'We need to work out a time we can all meet up again soon,' said Rose.

'Definitely,' said Jacob.

'You should all come to China,' suggested Jiao. 'An Unlisted excursion!'

Everyone laughed. 'Not tonight, Jiao. I'm wrecked,' said Dru, stifling a yawn.

'Me too,' said Kal. 'I gotta crash. Night, nerds!'

Kymara laughed as Kal moved away from the screen. 'Ha. Still working on those social skills, eh, Kal? Big love, everyone.' She signed off.

'See you!' said Jiao, cutting his connection.

'Schweet Duh-reams,' said Jacob.

'Night, guys,' said Gemma.

Then only Dru and Rose were left watching each other onscreen. 'Oh, right. Well, uh . . .'

'Ha. We miss you too, Dru. Take care,' said Rose.

Dru grinned. 'We did all right, didn't we?'

Rose nodded. 'Yeah. We did. G'night.'

The two friends waved to each other and Dru closed down the laptop. Kal was already lying in bed, yawning.

'So,' Dru said as he tucked himself in. 'Guess it's just us again.'

'*Shhh.* Twin one is trying to sleep,' muttered Kal.

'Infinity broke your brain, dude. *I'm* twin one,' Dru answered.

'You wish,' said Kal with a smile.

'Good to have you back. Night, bro,' said Dru.

'Night, Dru.' Kal turned off his bedside light.

As both boys closed their eyes, outside their partially open window a full moon glowed. Stars twinkled in the night sky. Everything was peaceful as the boys slowly drifted off to sleep.

Kal began breathing heavily, snuggled into his pillow, blissfully unaware of the tiny nanobot that had crawled through the window, making a beeline for Kal. It scuttled up the leg of the bed, across Kal's pillow and disappeared a moment later into his left ear.

Dru stirred, rubbed his nose, fluffed his pillow and then lay back down, falling asleep a moment later. One point five seconds after he stopped moving, a nanobot crawled up his neck and into his right ear.

ACKNOWLEDGEMENTS

The authors would like to thank Libby Doherty at the ABC and Bernadette O'Mahony at the Australian Children's Television Foundation for funding the development of *The Unlisted*; the talented screenwriters: Mithila Gupta, Tristram Baumber, Jane Allen, Timothy Lee, Natesha Somasundaram, Nicholas Brown, Rhys Graham and Greg Waters; Alice McCredie-Dando; the amazing team at Aquarius Films, Angie Fielder, Polly Staniford and Alice Willison, for taking on a high-end children's series for the first time and making it a fantastic experience from start to end; the cast and crew that helped to make it shine; and the ABC (again) and Netflix for screening it.

Thanks to the team at Hachette Australia for allowing us to re-live the whole story again on the page – in particular Brigid Mullane, Claire de Medici, Kate Flood and Sarah Brooks.

Our families put up with a lot during the sometimes fraught writing process, and we are ever grateful for their love and support.

XX Justine and Chris